PARIS ESCAPADE

A NOVEL BY
TED MYERS

Black Rose Writing | Texas

ISBN: 978-1-68433-595-4
PUBLISHED BY BLACK ROSE WRITING
www.blackrosewriting.com

Printed in the United States of America
Suggested Retail Price (SRP) $16.95

Paris Escapade is printed in Baskerville

*As a planet-friendly publisher, Black Rose Writing does its best to eliminate unnecessary waste to reduce paper usage and energy costs, while never compromising the reading experience. As a result, the final word count vs. page count may not meet common expectations.

PARIS ESCAPADE

I Even before we got on the plane, I was planning my getaway.

In June 1963, my seventeenth summer, my parents gave me a six-week camping trip in Europe. It was a reward for graduating high school. Not only did I graduate, I was Valedictorian. As impressive as that might sound, it was not. See, I had dropped out of the prestigious New York High School for the Arts after the first half of my senior year. I hated high school, just as I had hated junior high and grade school before that. I excelled only in the subjects that interested me: English, history, and art. As for math and science, I was terrible. I managed passing grades in biology and geometry, but when it came to chemistry and algebra, I foundered. I was just squeaking by in French. Because I had a good ear for music (by now I was playing folk music on my guitar in Washington Square and some of the minor coffeehouses), I mastered the pronunciation, which most of my classmates butchered. But all the many tenses and irregular verbs were more trouble than I wanted to put up with. I was an art major, so I got to do a lot of painting and drawing, and that was fun. But when I looked at the work of my peers, I knew that I would never be able to compete in the art world of New York City.

Besides, what I really wanted to do was write. I'd read the poetry of the Beats ("America...go fuck yourself with your atom bomb"), Arthur Rimbaud, two novels by Nikos Kazantzakis, the obligatory *Catcher in the Rye* (I thought Holden Caulfield was a dolt), *Crime and Punishment* (I really dug Raskolnikov), Terry Southern's *Candy* and *The Magic Christian*. The book I took along to read on the trip, *Cool City* by Nick duMornay, was up next. This was the story of Danny, a precocious Negro juvenile delinquent surviving the mean streets of Harlem. That book had created quite a buzz among the New York junior beatnik crowd.

Although I had access to all the white privilege Danny did not, and although I had not even read the book yet, I identified with that kid. He was an angry young man, and so was I. I was angry at anyone who had power over me. I was angry at the repressive society of America. Even though JFK had been in office for nearly three years now, to me it still felt like the '50s. I was in a hurry to grow up and move on, to escape the shackles of adult authority. So I dropped out of NYHSA after winter recess—to the horror of my parents, who are both teachers. I confess, I got a secret glee out of horrifying my parents, although they had never mistreated me in any way. They had committed no sin other than being normal and sensible and insufferably boring.

I got a minimum wage job at Mark Cross Ltd., makers of luxury gift items like silver-plated pen and pencil sets and diaries and address books bound in "fine morocco leather." Much of their business was mail order. My job was to translate the order blanks people had filled in and cut out from the Mark Cross catalog onto an official Mark Cross order form, which was then passed along to the Order Fulfillment Department. I lasted two weeks. Was this the working world? It was the most tedious two weeks of my life. Even worse than school.

My long-suffering parents found me a private school for underachievers called the Charles Dickens Academy. From the name, I envisioned an Oliver Twistian workhouse, but it wasn't like that at all. It was a repurposed brownstone on West 73rd Street, right off Central Park West. These were children of the wealthy who couldn't cut it in regular high school. Compared to them, I was a genius. To my surprise and delight, I found I had already completed the required amount of math, science, and language to get into most liberal arts colleges. So I only needed to take my easy subjects: English, history, art, and drama (we did a production of *Waiting for Godot* by Samuel Beckett—I played Estragon).

When they told me I was to be Valedictorian, it only confirmed what I'd already suspected: This school was a fraud, and there was nothing valid about being its Valedictorian. On graduation day, instead of getting all gussied up in a dark blue suit and reciting a bunch of starry-eyed platitudes for my sub-standard classmates, I played hooky. I simply didn't show up. I saved my parents the embarrassment of being there by telling them my plans ahead of time. They just shrugged and rolled their eyes. From me, they had seen it all; nothing more I could do could shock them. Or so they thought at the time.

I had been accepted by the only college I'd applied to, Chandler, a small enclave tucked away in the wilds of Vermont. What I had read about Chandler seemed to suit me to a tee: No grades, no exams, and you could dream up your own courses. It was somewhere to the left of progressive. So after the summer I would be heading north, perhaps never to live in my childhood home again. But perhaps I wouldn't even return from this trip.

We all gathered in the KLM waiting area at Idlewild International Airport. There were twenty-four of us. Our counselor would be meeting us on the other end: Amsterdam, Holland. His name was Art Rosen, an American professor who taught English at the University of Amsterdam. I didn't know any of the other kids, but as we waited to board our flight, we made small talk while sizing each other up. I mostly checked out the girls. There were a few who bordered on cute and one who, though not beautiful in the usual sense, attracted me enormously. She had straight, sandy-blonde hair, big blue eyes, and freckles. She also had a space between her front teeth that mitigated her otherwise-WASPy perfection. But mostly I liked that she was the least Jewish-looking person there.

See, the trip was sponsored by Camp Maplewood, a summer camp my parents had sent me to for several summers, starting from when I was about thirteen. It was a Jewish camp. Not in a religious way, but ethnically one hundred percent Jewish. Like my parents. Like my younger sister. Try as I might to distance myself from the Tribe, it enveloped me like chronic psoriasis. I refused to acknowledge my Jewishness. At thirteen, they made me get Bar Mitzvah'd, but I had not set foot inside a synagogue since then. That was one of the reasons I was in such a hurry to grow up and break free of my parents' world. They were not religious at all. In fact, they were agnostics. That whole charade of the Bar Mitzvah was unmitigated hypocrisy. But it goes deeper than that—well, it's a long story.

In keeping with my parents' sensible nature, we lived in a middle-class housing development in Manhattan called Stuyvesant Town. It was a project of the Metropolitan Life Insurance Company, built to alleviate the post-World War II housing crisis. We moved there in 1950 when I was four years old. We left the home of my paternal grandmother in the Bronx when my mother became pregnant with her second child, my little sister. My Grandma Sarah was my all-time favorite relative. She lavished on me more unreserved love than either of my parents. For some reason, my parents' capacity to demonstrate love had been stifled somewhere along the way. When I had to leave Grandma Sarah, I was heartbroken—and angry.

Stuyvesant Town was populated by other like-minded middle-class white people. There were no people of color. Roughly half the population was Jewish, and the other half was Catholic, mostly Irish. My parents only socialized with people of their own ilk: Jewish intellectuals, mostly teachers. They were all very sensible and bland. They all belonged to the same Reformed synagogue (code for "I don't believe in God but just want to hang out with my *lonsmen*"). They advocated sensible shoes, sensible career choices, sensible social choices. The scope of whom and whom not to associate with was extremely limited. So my upbringing was quite cloistered. Even the parents of my best friend, Arny Aronoff, were not educated well enough to be included in my parents' circle.

But once I turned thirteen, I broke loose. I started hanging out with Richie Downs, an inveterate juvenile delinquent with flaming red hair who lived on the far side of First Avenue, the equivalent of the other side of the tracks. Richie and I pulled some hair-raising pranks together. In retrospect, I'm surprised we didn't get anybody killed. Here's the story of our final stunt:

Richie always used to ride me around on his bike, which was his pride and joy. He was always tinkering with it, adding more gadgets. It was equipped with rearview mirrors, several headlights and taillights, and streamers at each end of the handlebars. He had even rigged a mount for his portable radio. He'd get on first, and then I'd hop onto the top tube sidesaddle and grab the middle of the handlebars with one hand.

The school year was winding down. It was June of 1959, and I was looking forward to going away to a co-ed summer camp (Maplewood). The radio played "Here Comes Summer" by Jerry Keller as Richie and I rode down to the East River one warm, sunny day. On one of the piers, about a dozen garbage trucks were parked in two lines. This was also the pier off which Richie and his buddies would go swimming. There were about six kids from Richie's neighborhood already in the water. Richie stripped down to his trunks and jumped in. I looked down at the murky brown water. There was no way I was going in there. My stomach turned at the thought of those idiots swimming through that slime. The kids had rigged a thick rope with knots every few feet that served as a ladder for them to climb back onto the pier. Richie climbed out and grabbed a towel he'd brought.

"Jeez, Richie, that's disgusting," I said.

"Nah, it's fine. Ya just have ta keep ya mouth closed."

Richie eyed the fleet of giant trucks. "I got a idea. Hey, Frankie, Joey, get up here! I got a idea!"

The other guys scrambled up the rope. Richie climbed up on the lead truck—the one closest to the river. He tried the doors, but they were locked. "Anybody know how to get in here?"

I stepped forward. "Lemme see your belt," I said.

The JDs would sharpen the edges of the buckles on their Garrison belts so they could be used as weapons in a rumble. The buckle on Richie's was filed so thin that I was able to slip it down into the crack between the window and the door. After some manipulation, I felt it catch on the door lock. I gave it a yank, and the driver's side door came unlocked. I opened the door and jumped down. All the guys clapped.

"The kid's got talent," said Joey Carbone, the biggest, oldest guy there.

It was the first time they had acknowledged my existence.

"Great," said Richie. He jumped into the driver's seat and released the emergency brake. He put the truck into neutral. "Everybody push!" he yelled. There were eight of us, seven pushing with all our might and Richie steering. How we got that forty-ton truck to start moving, I'll never know, but we did, and as it rolled, it gained momentum. When it reached the edge of the pier, Richie jumped out, and the hulking mass of gray steel plummeted into the East River, making the biggest splash I'd ever seen. We all cheered, feeling jubilant and victorious. But our celebration was short-lived. We heard the sirens approaching only moments after the truck hit the water.

The cops closed in from both north and south, blocking off any possible escape by land. All the boys—all except me—jumped into the river, but there was a police boat waiting to fish them out. My mind raced. I ducked under the nearest truck and ran between the two rows, praying the cops hadn't seen me. One of the trucks had a half-open window on the passenger side. I climbed up, shimmied through the window, and crouched down on the seat.

I poked my head up just for an instant, just long enough to see a cop wheeling Richie's bike away. The radio was still playing: "There Goes My Baby" by The Drifters. I huddled in the truck until it got dark, then I walked home.

I never saw Richie Downs again, and I never found out what happened to him. School let out a few days later, and I went off to camp. It seemed like every time I turned on the radio that summer, it played "There Goes My Baby," and it always made me think of Richie and wonder.

In 1959, the urban folk revival was in full swing. I had been taking guitar lessons since I turned thirteen. After learning a few folk songs and practicing in my room for a couple months, I felt confident enough to walk down to Greenwich Village on Sunday afternoons with my guitar in its brown canvas case slung over my shoulder to the Big Hootenanny in Washington Square. Hundreds of young people with guitars, banjos, mandolins, and *what-have-yous* would gather around the circular fountain near the Arch and form small ensembles. We would jam on all the folk standards that everybody knew: "Tom Dooley," "If I Had a Hammer," "Silver Dagger," and so on. Then there was the bluegrass set. Bluegrass was all about instrumental virtuosity. The songs themselves were very simplistic, so I could play the basic guitar accompaniment and sing the words and melody, but some of those banjo and mandolin cats could pick a mile a minute. They were the real stars.

Also around the Washington Square fountain was an assortment of non-musical Village characters: There was Leo C.V. Jones, a bushy-haired, bearded Negro guy about forty who would beat all the old men at chess, yelling "Checkmate, mothafucka!" at the top of his lungs. And then there was Tommy Fisk: About twenty, blond hair down to his shoulders, always trying to sell everybody "Black Beauties," amphetamine pills. But the thing I remember most about Tommy is when my high school girlfriend, Gina Giancarlo, started hanging around with him. Even though we had already broken up, I felt resentful and also fearful that he would get Gina hooked on speed.

At the same time, I had become an avid jazz fan. I joined the Columbia Records Club and received LPs by Dave Brubeck, Errol Garner, and Miles Davis. From there, I branched out to John Coltrane and Thelonious Monk. To me, the Negro giants of jazz were the epitome of cool. Although all I could do on guitar was play these simple folk songs, I resolved to become a jazz musician.

I talked my parents into buying me a used jazz guitar, a big, fat Gibson arch top electric and a small amp. I started taking lessons from an old jazz guitarist named Billy Bauer. He had played in Lenny Tristano's combo back in the 1940s. Every Saturday, I would take the subway up to West 48th Street, where Billy rented a cheap hotel room in which he would dispense guitar lessons. I was one of a stream of students parading in and out at half-hour intervals. The first thing I learned was scales, the major and the various modes of minor. I learned how to position my left hand on the guitar neck so as to play any scale in any key. I also learned many new chords; major, minor, augmented, diminished. But then he tried to teach me how to read music. Apparently, this was a must if you wanted to play jazz. And that's where he lost me. Trying to translate those little dots on the staff into actual sounds was simply too hard for me. It was like math or learning to read a new language. My brain simply didn't work that way. Billy made the mistake of writing out a simple melody for me to play, then playing it for me. As soon as he played it, I played it right back to him,

7

pretending to read the notes. My excellent ear was my undoing. And that's how I screwed myself out of learning to read music.

Being at the age of having more self-confidence than was warranted, I insinuated myself into the Negro jazz musician crowd at school and soon was schlepping my guitar and amp out to Jimmy Hunter's house in the all-Negro Brooklyn neighborhood of Bedford Stuyvesant.

Amazingly, I—a skinny white kid with an electric guitar and amp—passed unmolested through those streets many times. Jimmy was a big, goofy, good-natured guy with black-rimmed glasses. Not a brilliant conversationalist, but a truly gifted jazz pianist. There was also John Cruz on alto sax (not gifted, but a game trier) and a revolving cast of other horn players, bass players, and drummers. Sometimes I would bring my white drummer friend, Fred. Fred was part of the uptown preppy set I ran with occasionally. They were all children of the rich and famous in Manhattan. Fred's mother was a glamorous Park Avenue divorcee from North Carolina. As unlikely a jazz hippie as he looked in his blue blazer, school tie, and khaki slacks, Fred was a serious and talented drummer. Besides, he had a car. There's no way we could've gotten to Bed Stuy with electric guitar, amp, and a full set of drums on the subway.

We played a wide array of the best of the modern jazz that was popular at the time: Horace Silver, Art Blakey, and, of course, Miles. Somehow I was able to follow along most of the time, although I can't say my guitar playing added much to the overall gestalt.

My art skills finally came in handy when I learned to forge the New York State driver's license. This consisted of a flimsy green slip of paper that was torn off your driver's license application. The only thing that made it an official driver's license was the New York State seal stamped in a box in the upper right corner. You could grab as many application forms as you wanted at the Dept. of Motor Vehicles, and eventually I perfected drawing the rubber-stamped seal with a black ballpoint pen. I made fake IDs for all my "jazz hippie" friends (jazz hippie just means someone who's hip to jazz). We made the rounds of all the New York jazz clubs: The Five Spot, the Half Note, the Blue Note, the Jazz Gallery, Birdland, the Village Gate, and the Village Vanguard. It was usually dark enough where they checked the IDs so that no one ever busted us. At the time, the drinking age in New York was eighteen, so we weren't conspicuously young. We got to see all the greats live: Coltrane, Miles, Monk, Art Blakey's Jazz Messengers, Herbie Mann, Nina Simone, and many others.

But when I dropped out of NYHSA, all this came to an end. Besides, by the time I started at Charles Dickens, I'd decided to become a writer anyway. A writer living in a garret on the Left Bank in Paris.

II On the plane, I sat next to Robin, the freckle-faced, blue-eyed, gap-toothed, very-white girl, the most shiksa-looking girl on the trip. I got in early to stake my claim. There would be at least four weeks of roaming around Europe before we hit Paris, and I wanted to make that part of the journey as pleasurable as possible. The attraction seemed to be mutual, and the eleven-hour journey (including a refueling stop in Shannon, Ireland) promised to pass quite pleasantly. Robin Reichenbach. That was her name. Very Teutonic-sounding, but she was Jewish alright.

"So, Robin," I said, wracking my brain for something interesting to say, "your family lives in Queens?"

"Long Island. East Hampton."

"Snazzy. You goin' to college in the fall?"

"Yeah. I got into Cooper Union. I'm an artist."

"No kidding? I was an art student as well. I went to New York High School of the Arts."

"Wow. I wish I had gone there, but we live too far away. I mean, I'd have to get up at four in the morning to commute to Manhattan every day from the Island."

"Yeah, I see what you mean. I'm sure you would've gotten in, though. Cooper Union, that's *major*."

"Yeah. I'm excited." She gave a cute little laugh. Her smile—gap-tooth notwithstanding—was charming. She asked me about my art, and I regaled her with basically the story of my life: how I had given up on art and gotten into music and then given up on music and how I was now gonna be a writer. I almost said, "In a garret on the Left Bank in Paris," but thankfully I stifled myself.

It was my first time on an airplane. I had never had occasion to travel far enough from New York to need one. I was filled with excitement and anticipation—The Great Unknown.

When the pilot announced that we were free to move about the cabin, I got up and spoke with a few of the other campers. One boy, Johnny Barron, struck me as a fellow rebel. He had straight, even features, dark hair, and he seemed to be working on the beginnings of a goatee. He confirmed this as soon as we started talking. He also sported brown leather sandals. "I hear you can buy good ones really cheap in Italy," I said.

"Well, maybe I'll buy a second pair."

"I'm gonna get sandals in *Italia*, and in *la France* I'm gonna get a boat neck with blue and white horizontal stripes."

"Ah oui?"

"Mais, certainement!"

"Moi, je vais acheter un béret."

I complimented him on his accent.

"Yeah, you too," he said.

"I don't know too many words, mais mon accent, c'est magnifique!"

We had a good laugh, then he said, *sotto voce*, "Hey, who's the girl?" With a flick of his bristly chin, he indicated Robin, seated several rows ahead.

"*Rrrobin Rrreichenbach*," I said, growling my 'r's in an exaggerated German accent and clicking my heels.

"Not bad," he whispered. "Is she really Jewish?"

"Yeah, that's what I said. But she is. Definitely. Alas." We had another laugh, and I moved on.

A few aisles aft, I was accosted by a dark-haired, bespectacled girl.

"Hey, come ova hea. I wanna tawk ta you," she said in an accent as thick as the Brooklyn phone book.

She was petite and had a nice shape. Without the glasses, which were framed in black-rimmed teardrops (the standard feminine eyewear), she would've been downright cute. But she embodied everything I was trying to run away from: loud, pushy, and completely devoid of mystery. If a Gentile said these were Jewish traits, I'd be offended and say they were stereotyping. But I'm saying them, and it's because I know it's true. She grabbed my wrist and pulled me into the seat beside her.

11

"Hi, what's your name?"

"I'm Eddie. Eddie Strull. And you are…?"

"Evelyn Feinberg. You can call me Evy. Hey, Evy and Eddie. It rhymes!"

"Yeah," I said flatly. "What part of New York you from?" I knew she was going to say it.

"Brooklyn. Bensonhurst. Hey, how come you wear your hair so long?"

"I'm a beatnik."

"Yeah? You ever hang out in The Village?"

"All the time. It's my home away from home, so to speak. I can walk there from my parents' house."

"No kiddin'. That's cool!" I was out of conversation. I looked toward the front of the plane. There was a brown cowlick protruding above the back of my seat. There was some tall person sitting next to Robin.

"Hey, I'll talk to you later, okay? See ya later."

I got up and walked toward my row. The guy in my seat had straight brown hair and disgustingly symmetrical features. The white tennis sweater pretentiously draped around his shoulders, sleeves tied at the neck, made him look more like an uptown preppy than a graduate of Midwood High School in Brooklyn, which is what he was.

"Hi," I said, holding out my hand, "I'm Eddie." He looked away and whispered something in Robin's ear. They both laughed. I felt a rush of heat in my face. *I will stay calm, I will stay calm.* My hand was still outstretched.

"Eddie Strull," I said pointedly. "That's my name."

"Michael Phillips," he said, limply shaking my hand.

"This is my seat," I said.

"Oh yeah? Your name on here somewhere?" He made a comical show of examining the seat for my nameplate. Robin giggled. "I thought we were 'circulating.'" He made air quotes and gave me a scornful smile.

"Yeah. *Were.* Past tense. And now I'd like my seat back." I smiled daggers at him. He leaned over and whispered something else to Robin. She smiled and nodded. Then he got up, ever so slowly, and returned to his seat, deliberately bumping me as he passed. I sat down.

"You actually *like* that guy?"

"Well, I did find him quite charming."

"Yeah. His charm oozed all over me. I feel like taking a shower."

12

"Jealousy doesn't become you, Eddie Strull. Besides, it's a little early to get possessive, wouldn't you say?"

Of course she was right. I looked at her sheepishly, then looked down. Then she kissed me on the cheek. It was so unexpected, I nearly jumped. There must have been a comical look on my face, because she was laughing.

Night falls quickly when you're flying with the Earth's rotation and the sun's going the other way. Robin fell asleep first, and gradually her head rested on my shoulder. It felt good. I fell asleep feeling somewhat reassured, but the balance of power in our budding relationship had definitely shifted.

We awoke when the pilot announced we were about to land at Shannon airport for a fifteen-minute refueling stop. It was broad daylight, and the last leg of our flight would be brief, so we didn't bother going back to sleep. An hour later, we landed at Schiphol airport. It was ten in the morning, Amsterdam time. We were met on the tarmac by Art, our senior counselor, a pleasant-looking man of about thirty, and our two junior counselors, Gerard (pronounced *Herart*) and Tini. They were college-age, maybe nineteen or twenty, both very blond and really good-looking.

After collecting our suitcases, knapsacks, and sleeping bags, we had to pass through customs. All the Dutch customs inspectors were smiling and friendly. Outside the terminal, we boarded the bus that would take us through seven countries in six weeks. We learned how to say hello in Dutch to our bus driver, Job (pronounced *Yope*). "Hoi, Job."

The weather was cool, gray, and overcast, which suited me fine, considering the usual summer weather in New York City: Ninety degrees temperature, ninety percent humidity.

We spent a few days in Amsterdam, a city of canals and bicycles. While tooling around the city on our rented bikes, we noticed the curious custom girls had of holding hands while walking together. This gave rise to the crack that "there are more dykes in Holland than we'd imagined."

After a couple of day trips to Rotterdam and The Hague, we each spent three nights with a Dutch family. Mine was the Beenhouwers. Everybody in Holland, it seemed, spoke English really well and the Beenhouwers were no exception. There was a mother, a father, and two sons. The older boy, Bas, was about a year older than I. Blond (of course) with glasses. They lived in a town called Noordwijk, in the southwest, right on the ocean. There were actual dykes to keep the ocean out. Bas took me touring on his moped, a motor scooter with pedals. I had never been on a motorized two-wheel vehicle, and the sensation was quite exhilarating—the sea-sprayed wind whistling through our hair and all around us and a marvelous illusion of speed. Something close, I thought, to flying. I learned two words in Dutch: *fietje* (bicycle) and *broomfietje* (motorcycle). The other thing that stands out in my memory is the buttered toast with chocolate sprinkles for breakfast. Wonderful butter; wonderful chocolate. Great country, Holland.

On the third day, the bus, already mostly filled with campers, came to pick me up. I invited Bas to stay with my family when he came to America (this was the accepted protocol). *Good luck with my parents*, I thought, *'cause I won't be there*. I bade farewell to the Beenhouwers and boarded. And there they were: Robin and Michael Phillips sitting side-by-side. My spirits suddenly plummeted. They were toward the back, deep in conversation. Robin did not seem to notice me. Evy gave me a wan smile and waved.

"Sit here, Eddie." It was Johnny, whose reddish goatee was coming in nicely. I stowed my knapsack on the shelf above and sat down next to him. It was probably for the best, I told myself. No sense forming any strong attachments. Next stop: Bruges, Belgium.

We continued south along the coast of the North Sea, taking a causeway that crossed as much water as land. We reached the Belgian border very soon. It was like driving from New York to New Jersey. At the border, we all had to get out and have our passports stamped. When we re-boarded, Robin got on ahead of me and seated herself in an aisle seat near the front. When I walked by, she grabbed my arm and pulled me into the seat beside her. "Hello, stranger," she said.

I smiled and sang my reply: "'Seems like a mighty long time…'"

She joined in: "'Sh-bop, sh-bop, my baby ooh.'" It was a record by Barbara Lewis that was all over the American radio that summer. Our eyes met, and we dissolved in laughter. Then she hugged me. My emotions ran riot, bouncing off each other like pugnacious billiard balls. I wanted to resist, I wanted to make her pay for making me suffer, I wanted to feel nothing, I was sure she would stab me in the back again, I wanted to hold her like this forever.

Bruges is an ancient city in the northwest of Belgium, close to the sea. We camped out for two nights in a public campground just outside of town. Camp Maplewood provided two-man pup tents, and we had our own sleeping bags. I shared a tent with Johnny, who was so far the only boy I had befriended.

The town was like a toy replica of a medieval village. The spotless, cobbled streets and perfectly preserved thirteenth-century buildings could have been an attraction at Disneyland. Gothic Churches with extravagant murals, stained glass, and gilded statues. We would see quite a lot of these in the coming weeks. More canals with quaint little bridges. And swans, lots of swans. Everybody snapped pictures like mad with their Brownies. A few had good cameras, but I had a Brownie and felt obligated to join in the snapping—evidence to show my parents I had actually been there. If I ever saw them again.

At night, we gathered around a big campfire. We were joined by other young people from all over the world who were touring Europe with sleeping bags and knapsacks, just as so many kids had done for countless summers before. Some of them had guitars and other instruments. We sang songs from America, England, Germany, France, Sweden. I spoke with people from all over Europe and several from Japan. I learned words from other languages and taught them hip new American phrases, like "What's happening, baby?" ("Qu'est qui s'passe, bébé?").

When everyone headed back to their tents, Robin and I snuck off into the woods. We wandered through the beech- and oak-canopied forest. There was no sound but the wind gently rustling the trees and the crunch of dead leaves under our feet. It smelled like some woods from my past (a summer place in upstate New York?), like a beckoning mystery. We soon came to a grassy field that sloped downward toward a stream or canal.

Below, in the near distance, there were a few lights visible from houses. We sat looking over the moonlit landscape. Robin had her own unique scent. Thankfully, she didn't wear perfume. Her clothes smelled of smoke from the campfire. Both of us did. But, as I kissed her neck, her skin had a scent that reminded me of pine sap and vanilla. It aroused me tremendously. We faced each other and kissed.

First kisses are so important. If you're really paying attention, they can tell you everything you need to know about a person and what your relationship is going to be. Her lips, her tongue, her breath…they transported me to another dimension. A place I'd never been. We lay down in the grass and pressed our bodies together. We were a perfect fit. I could only imagine what this would be without clothes, but alas, Robin was certainly a virgin, and neither of us was ready to cross that line. Of course, I had my own secret reasons. This episode was causing me considerable confusion and thinking about it gave me a headache.

"Hey, you two!" A flashlight beam fell upon us. It was Art, our head caretaker. Robin and I sprung apart like the north poles of two magnets. "What're you doing? We've been looking all over for you!" He sounded more agitated than I had ever heard him.

"Nothing. We just took a walk," I said.

"Well, from now on, there's no wandering off without telling me." Then he yelled something in Dutch, and Gerard and Tini materialized from opposite sides of the field. The two junior counselors looked at us, exchanged a crack, and laughed. Art said something stern that shut them up.

We all returned to the campsite without further conversation. Suddenly, Art and his minions became my new enemies.

Wait until I disappear, I thought, *you'll have a lot of explaining to do.*

When I entered the tent, Johnny was waiting up for me with a big grin. "Well, did you score?"

"No, and I wouldn't tell anybody if I had," I said.

I had learned the summer I was thirteen that kind of braggadocio led only to disaster. That was my first summer at Camp Maplewood. I was there for the first six weeks of the summer, then I joined my parents and kid sister at a bungalow colony north of New York City for the last two weeks of the summer. I learned a lot about girls that summer.

While at camp, we went on a bus trip to the Tanglewood Music Festival in Stockbridge, Massachusetts. It was a long drive. I sat next to a girl named Louise. She was not very pretty but had a nice body and reputation for being "fast." At some point, it got dark and we started making out. She showed me how to French kiss and even let me put my hand under her blouse and feel her up (under the shirt, but over the bra). That night in my sleeping bag, I learned what guys meant by the term "blue balls."

After camp at the bungalow colony, I met Laura Hunt, by far the prettiest girl in the place. They held dances in the rec hall on Saturday nights. One night, to my amazement, Laura asked me to walk her home. Her parents owned their own house on a hill that bordered the bungalow colony. The parents were not home—probably still at the dance. We turned on the radio and sat on the couch. She let me put my arm around her. Before long, I got up the nerve to kiss her—and she kissed me back. I was smitten. I left her house dizzy with anticipation; Laura Hunt was going to be my girlfriend. Of course, I had to tell someone. So I told Stevie Moshman, swearing him to secrecy, and he told his little sister, and she told *everybody*. And when it got back to Laura, she never spoke to me again. I grieved over that misstep the whole rest of the summer, and I never forgot the lesson: Kiss and tell at your own peril.

We went next to Ghent, which is a lot like Bruges; ancient, pristine, watery. On the bus, I sat with Johnny. Robin sat with a bedraggled dishrag of a girl called Marla, whom she had befriended, perhaps out of pity. I had decided to distance myself from Robin for the duration. I was hellbent on following through with my disappearing act, and I could see further attachment would only weaken my resolve.

After a day or two of looking at more medieval architecture, churches, museums—objects of art and worship so exquisite, it boggled the mind to think they were made by human hands—we headed for Germany. We were to go to Cologne (Köln) and Munich (München), with a stop in-between at the infamous concentration camp, Dachau. Outside the window, the verdant German summer flew by.

The boy across the aisle from me, Jeffrey Burger, was reading a book about the Nazis and concentration camps and holding forth to all who would listen about the unspeakable cruelties, the ovens, the starvation, the medical experiments in lurid detail. He had studied German in school, and he was anxious to try it out on some real Germans. "They have very strict laws now about antisemitism," he was saying, "stricter than in the U.S. They want to make sure nothing like that ever happens again."

I had been hearing about the murder of six million Jews in concentration camps all my life. It was ingrained in the Jewish psyche. I had no relatives that I knew of who were in concentration camps—my grandparents and great-grandparents had come to America in the late nineteenth century—but I had met plenty of people whose family members had died or lived through that horror. I had heard so many of these stories that I believed I had become inured to the whole thing. I understood the evil of it but distanced myself emotionally. Now we were going to see where it happened, and I felt uneasy.

In Cologne, we saw a grand Gothic cathedral with two high spires and an art museum that had some very good Picassos. I was starting to burn out on churches and museums. We camped at a public campsite halfway between Cologne and Dachau.

That night, Robin came to my tent. I asked Johnny to leave us alone for a few minutes, and he obliged. "What's wrong?" she asked. "Have I done something to offend you?"

"No, of course not." I wracked my brain for something to say, something that would sound credible and not upset her. "It's just that... I have someone back home I promised to be faithful to. And I'm afraid that, if we kept on the way we were going, I would break my promise. So I think it would be best if we..."

"Oh." Her voice was taut with anger. "Why didn't you tell me before that walk in the woods that got us in so much trouble and everybody talking about us?"

"I'm sorry. I should have. I'm very attracted to you, Robin. I didn't know how much until the other night."

"Fine. I'm not going to say we can be friends, because we can't. From now on, my reputation is shot around here—and yours, I'm sure, is soaring. You're the Don Juan, and I'm the slut!"

"I never meant for that to happen. If anyone asked me, I've said nothing happened between us."

"Very gall*ant* of you, I'm sure." She started to cry and stormed out of the tent. My stomach was in a knot. I had that hollow feeling in my chest that comes when you've lost something irreplaceable.

After a couple of sunny days, the sky reverted to its pearly gray patina, with the sun trying in vain to break through. The weather reflected my mood as we reached Dachau.

It had been preserved as a memorial and holocaust museum. We got a guided tour of the place. We walked through the iron entrance gate with the famous sign over it, ARBEIT MACHT FREI, the austere wooden barracks, the infamous showers-cum-gas chambers, and, of course, the ovens. These were a bunch of stolid redbrick cubes clustered at the center of a large shed. Each had an arch-shaped door just about waist-high. You could easily slide a prone body in there, especially if it was emaciated from starvation and light as a feather. At last, the enormity of the evil that was done here permeated my heart and I had to hide the tears that I suddenly realized were dribbling down my cheeks. A few of the other kids were crying too as the tour guide explained in excruciating detail how the executions and cremations were carried out.

Next, we went to Munich; more ancient buildings, palaces, parks, museums, and a beer hall that had been open for 400 years. I'd had enough of sightseeing. I was anxious to get it all over with. To get to Paris and disappear.

Robin was still very cold and distant. She never made eye contact. The thought of seeing her like this every day for the next four weeks depressed me terribly. On the bus, she always sat with either Marla or Michael

Phillips. Was she nurturing a new romance? That thought depressed me even more.

Now, we were headed to Austria. First, Vienna and a concert by the Vienna Philharmonic at the famous Musikverein. But it was Strauss waltzes—ugh! Then, up into the Tyrolian Alps. Beautiful countryside, vast, green meadows, quaint Tyrolian towns, rich, creamy desserts "mit schlag." The waitresses always asked if we wanted ours mit schlag (with whipped cream) and we always said, "Ya."

By now, everyone had settled into a habitual seat. I sat with Johnny, Jeffrey Burger sat across the aisle, and somewhere behind us, Robin sat with Michael Phillips. Jeffrey had picked up a copy of the New York Herald-Tribune in Vienna, and Johnny and Jeffrey were talking enthusiastically about the progress of the New York Yankees. As usual, the Yankees dominated the American League, while the Los Angeles Dodgers were wracking up an impressive season in the National League. One of the main subjects of conversation on the bus was the spectacular left-handed pitcher for the Dodgers, Sandy Koufax, who was Jewish. When I was a kid, I was a Brooklyn Dodgers fan—"the Brooklyn Bums," the perennial underdogs—but since they had moved to L.A. in 1957, abandoning their New York fans, I had renounced them in disgust. I'd always hated the Yankees because they had so much money, they could buy all the best players in the league, always winning every year. So I mostly sat the conversation out, having nothing good to say about either team.

Next, we crossed a significant border, into communist Yugoslavia. We expected dismal, gray, dilapidated buildings like you'd see in the newsreels of East Berlin, but Yugoslavia was beautiful. Green, steep hills, medieval castles, a cosmopolitan, sophisticated city (Ljubljana), and terrific restaurants. The language was so alien—even the alphabet—that I had to stand in front of the restrooms and wait until someone came out to tell the men's from the ladies'. Yugoslavia was controlled by Tito, the "jolly dictator." Tito was more benevolent than the other Eastern European dictators, and less a lackey of the Russians. He ran his country his way, and apparently the people were pretty happy about it.

Next, *la bella Italia*. We made our way down the Adriatic Coast to Venice. Now, the weather had turned hot and sunny. On the bus, the seating arrangements had changed, as both Johnny and Jeffrey had now acquired female companions. Johnny had Carol: dark and thin with bright, birdlike eyes and a beak-like nose. She had a ready wit and a bon mot for almost everything. Lucy, Jeffrey's pick, was very quiet, short, had black brillo hair and a cute face. I was now relegated to an empty aisle seat next to my old pal, Evy, who talked incessantly about nothing. I tried to read or sleep, but it was no use.

It turned out Evy was Queen of the Malapropism. She would punctuate her nonstop flow of banalities with "so, at any rape..." But the best one was when we were gawking at some early Christian relics inside an old church. She said, "What's all this fuss about the Virgin Murry?"

Venice, although crawling with tourists, was alive with a kind of *joie de vivre* that was infectious, and my mood lifted. I tagged along with Johnny, Jeffrey, and their newly acquired girlfriends. Evy glommed onto us. Glommed onto *me*, to be more precise. I didn't resist; she was obnoxious, but at least there was no danger of emotional entanglement. We wandered the narrow winding streets, bought leather sandals, lounged in the cafes, and rode in gondolas through the labyrinth of canals. The food was great, and the people were cheerful and friendly. Carol kept us in stitches constantly (q: "What's a specimen?" a: "An Italian astronaut"). What a panic she was—a welcome distraction from my thoughts, which were dark and dismal and filled with doubt. Every now and then I would catch a glimpse of Robin walking with Michael, and the gloom would close in again.

We camped on the Lido, a narrow strip of sand in the Venetian Lagoon. The campsite had a snack bar with a paved patio for dancing. There were lovely colored lanterns strung from poles, and they served beer and wine, as well as snacks. At night, all the young campers from every country would come together and dance. They played many records I didn't recognize, like "Lucky Lips" by Cliff Richard, and some that I did, like "Volare" by Domenico Modugno. One particular favorite was "It's Now or Never" by Elvis Presley. I found out the English lyrics were put to an old Neapolitan melody, "'O Sole Mio," so the Italians loved it. I always thought it was "Oh Solo Mio," a self-pitying lament by a guy who was all alone (solo means alone, right?), but no. It's "sole," and it translates roughly to "you are my sunshine."

I danced with girls from Germany, France, England, and Brazil. And Italian girls. Ah, the Italian girls. I spoke French with a French couple and found that I could speak and understand quite well on a rudimentary level. They were very tolerant and corrected my errors; not like the haughty French everyone speaks about. Everybody seemed to like Americans.

One guy had a guitar, and after much prodding, I regaled them with "If I Had a Hammer," a well-known folk song in the U.S., but that year it was an international hit by Trini Lopez, so everybody knew it and sang along in their various accents.

One balmy night, a few of us went swimming in the tepid, shallow water of the Adriatic. You could walk out 500 feet and still be no more than waist-deep. Evy and I frolicked in the calm wavelets and ended up embracing. I was turned on by the feel of her warm, wet body against mine in spite of myself. After that, she considered herself my girlfriend whether I liked it or not. I neither encouraged nor discouraged her. The next day, I caught Robin looking at us once or twice with a baleful expression on her face.

We followed the Adriatic coast southward, stopping at Padua to see Giotto's celebrated frescoes and Ravenna to see the mosaics. Then inland through the undulating hills of Tuscany to Florence, where a magical golden light permeates everything and you see what inspired the world's greatest works of art. We sat at cafés in the Piazza San Marco, drinking Cokes and *acqua minerale*, went to the Uffizi gallery, the Ponte Vecchio, the Duomo, and the Galleria dell'Accademia to see Michelangelo's David. Carol speculated that his penis was probably pilfered from a much smaller statue.

We camped in the hills, where we had a panoramic view of the city. The first night, Evy tried to crawl into my sleeping bag with me. She didn't even care that Johnny was not two feet away, pretending to sleep and trying like hell to stifle his laughter.

"Are you crazy?" I yelled in a whisper. "You're gonna get us all in trouble." And I kicked her out.

The next day, we headed south to Rome. It was a long haul, more than three hours. Well, maybe not so long, but sitting next to Evy, it certainly seemed that way. As usual, she talked a lot of nonsense, and I just nodded my head while reading *Cool City* and pretended to be listening. But then she leaned forward and whispered something in my ear that got my attention: "Ever have a blowjob?"

I turned to her. "Huh? No."

"Would you like one? I'm really good at it."

"Sure. But it won't mean I'm going steady with you or anything, okay?"

"Okay."

"Where can we do it?"

"Right here!"

"Are you kidding?" And before I could say another word, she leaned over and unzipped my fly. I looked across the aisle nervously. The only places from which we could be seen were three rows opposite us, the one directly across, the one ahead, and the one behind. All I saw were sleeping heads. I held my book on my left thigh as a shield. By this time, she had it in her mouth—and then, *bam!* It was all over.

"Thanks a lot," I whispered, "that was wonderful."

"Oh, that's okay," she said, spitting my semen into a Kleenex. "Just a small token of my steam."

I was not completely inexperienced. In New York, I ran with a fast crowd, and twice I'd had fumbling, drunken sex with people I hardly knew and cared nothing about. But as ditsy as Evy was, she had conferred on me an act of selfless affection, and I had to appreciate her for that.

"You're crazy, you know that?" I said.

"Yeah. I get that a lot."

In Rome, we toured all the requisite sights: The Colosseum, the Sistine Chapel, the ruins of the Forum, etc. We stayed in a youth hostel for three nights; the toilet paper was newspaper cut into small squares. But what made the greatest impression on me in Italy were the Italians. One afternoon, we were wandering some of the narrow backstreets of Rome, looking in shops. The girls wanted to buy some of those dangling earrings that were in vogue that year. The man in the shop spoke English and loved Americans. When we asked him where was the best place to eat around here, he was so anxious to turn us on to his favorite restaurant, he closed the shop and took us there himself. He sat with us and recommended the best dishes, ordering for us in Italian. Great country, Italy.

After Rome, we worked our way up the Mediterranean coast, stopping at Pisa to see the Leaning Tower and at some of the beach towns like Viareggio, where we rented small sailboats. We sailed out a few hundred yards, then took down the sails and dove into the crystal-blue water. Then, swinging up and around into the Côte d'Azur: Monaco, Nice, Cannes, and Saint-Tropez, where we swam, ate wonderful food, and camped on beaches.

In Saint-Tropez, we laid ourselves out on towels on the hot, sandy beach. After a while, I got up and walked toward the snack bar to use the bathroom. That's when I saw her: Bright red bikini, broad-brimmed straw hat, long, auburn hair, hoop earrings, white-framed sunglasses. She lowered the sunglasses and looked right at me. It was an unmistakable invitation. In the bathroom, I resolved to speak to her. I walked over and said, "Bonne après-midi! Je m'appelle Eddie."

Her name was Martisse. She was older than me—at least nineteen— and I was sure she was out of my league, but she was very friendly. We hung out together on her beach blanket. She spoke English about as well as I spoke French, so we helped each other, limping along in our broken dialects, wantonly wrecking each other's native tongue. Martisse did wonderful things for a French bikini—and more than once I caught Robin glaring at us across the sand. The American girls wore two-piece suits, but the pieces were much larger, and the space between much smaller. I asked her where she called home. Paris, *rive gauche*. She said she was studying art at the Sorbonne and earned her living as a model for other artists (ooh la la!). She was returning home in a week, leaving tomorrow for Marseille to visit family. The timing seemed more than propitious. I told her I would be in Paris in three or four days, and she gave me her address and phone number, urging me to contact her next week.

The snack bar had a paved patio with round tables shaded by *Cinzano* umbrellas. It was very hot on the sand, so I invited her to join me for a Coke, and we adjourned to a shaded table. Evy, oblivious to decorum as always, invited herself to join us and made me introduce her to Martisse and buy her a Coke. When her Coke arrived, Evy smiled at Martisse. "Gee, you're pretty."

Martisse looked at me questioningly. I translated: "Elle a dit que vous étais très jolie."

"Merci beaucoup," said Martisse.

"I gave him a blowjob on the bus," said Evy, still smiling idiotically at her.

Martisse looked at me again. "Q'est ce que c'est 'blowjob'?"

"Rien," I said. "Evy, get the hell out of here before I kill you." I said this very quietly, barely moving my lips. Evy fled. Martisse took it all in with amusement.

"Mais, dit moi: What is blowjob?"

"Ça ne fait rien." (It's nothing.)

Now I was more impatient than ever to get to *la belle Paris*.

Back on the bus, Johnny and Jeffrey pulled me aside, away from the girls. "I don't know how you do it, man," Johnny said in a loud whisper.

"Do what?"

Jeff chimed in, "You know, that French babe. Man, what a knockout! What does she see in you?"

"Nothing much, I'm sure. I think she was just being friendly to a foreigner."

"Oh, sure. First Robin, now this." They laughed with a mixture of admiration and envy. Truth be told, I had never been that popular with girls. I'd never had much of what they call "animal magnetism." I guess maybe something about Europe, about hearing and speaking foreign languages, brought it out of me. Or maybe I was just growing up.

I went back to my seat next to Evy. We headed northwest, bypassing Marseille, to Lyon, then Chartres to see the famous cathedral (beaucoup des flying buttresses) and after three more days, seven cathedrals, four museums, and twelve amazing restaurants—Paris. I insisted on switching places with Evy to be near the window. My eyes were glued to the passing view: First, a series of suburbs, nothing much to see there. Then, we were in the city proper. From the main road, Quai de la Rapée, which followed the Seine, I could see the ancient maze of old buildings, slanted rooftops, chimneys jutting here and there, narrow side streets, broad boulevards. The Eifel Tower came into view, then the Arc de Triomphe.

We stayed at a youth hostel on rue Lamarck in the Montmartre district, a steep street close to the summit, the white-domed Sacré Coeur, the beating heart of Paris. It was late afternoon when we arrived, so just enough time to get settled in and get ready for dinner. Johnny and I shared a dorm-like space with Jeffrey and another boy in our party, Peter Hochman. We had to tidy up and look a bit presentable, as Art was taking us to a really nice restaurant, Le Bon Bock, the oldest restaurant in Montmartre. As evening fell, we walked down the hill (*le Butte*) through crowds of tourists. I heard no French; just English and German. The entire city was spread out beneath us like a box of candy.

The decor at Le Bon Bock was ornate, essentially unchanged since the place opened in 1879. The high walls were covered with old paintings, all from the pre-impressionist era. There was a bar stocked with a towering array of exotic beverages. The food was excellent and not too expensive. I had a salmon dish with a wonderful creamy sauce, little potatoes, and asparagus. The waiters were friendly and polite, not snotty and superior as I expected. I suppose it was because their main clientele were foreigners. It helped that Art spoke French well and Johnny and I both ordered in French. They like it when you make an effort.

I couldn't help glancing at Robin, who sat at a neighboring table with Michael and Marla, the dishrag girl. She saw me looking and returned my glance with something in her eyes I could only interpret as sadness.

When we got back to the dorm room, Johnny, Jeffrey, Peter, and I decided to ask Art if we could go to the Folies Bèrgere tomorrow night. We had heard they let kids our age in, no problem, and the girls all walked and danced around the stage *topless*. The next day, we asked, and Art said yes! Maybe he wasn't such an *oeuf dur* (tough cookie) after all.

And so, the next night, we dressed in our fanciest duds (jackets and ties) and polished our shoes. After studying a map, we discovered Montmartre and rue Richer, where the Folies was, were both in the 9th arrondissement and we would get there quicker if we walked than if we took the métro. Plus, we would get to see a bit of Paris at night. The shortest route was just 1.8 kilometers, a little over a mile. The first show was at nine, and we started out, map in hand, at eight p.m.

We had to follow a somewhat circuitous route to find rue des Martyrs, which was the main thoroughfare we would follow most of the way. But we must have taken a wrong turn, because we found ourselves on a dark, narrow street. And on that street was a bar, and out of that bar came four dodgy-looking characters, yelling drunkenly and pushing each other into garbage cans. They were young but bigger and older than us. When they spotted us, one of them yelled something in French. It sounded to me like an obscenity, followed by "Give us your money." The last word was *argent*, so it was pretty easy to fill in what came before. Now, I don't know about the others, but I had quite a lot of money on me. I had secretly sold the coin collection left to me by my grandfather for $500 before leaving New York, and I converted it all into traveler's checks to finance my disappearing act. Of this, I had around 200 francs in cash on me. The four guys were now running toward us. When they were almost upon us, I turned and picked up an empty trash can and threw it at them. It tripped them up, but only for a second. "Run!" I yelled, and we all took off running toward the bright lights of a big boulevard dead ahead. "Maybe we can get a taxi there," I said. The hooligans were hot on our trail but significantly slowed by drunkenness. We made it to rue des Martyrs and I ran right out into traffic, waving my arms crazily, and almost got run over by a taxi. It was vacant. The cabbie picked us up, and we were off to *Les Follies*. The Gang of Four ran after the cab, throwing tin cans and garbage at us. The last thing I heard was "Sales américains!" (Dirty Americans).

The show was squeaky-clean. What a disappointment. Somehow they managed to make beautiful girls walking around topless not sexy. All the performers, male and female, had perfect bodies. Lots of body makeup to cover all blemishes and even mitigate nipples. The choreography was mainly quasi-ballet moves; shirtless guys in tights lifting and twirling girls in nothing but bikini bottoms and toe shoes. There was a big production number of "La Vie en Rose," with girls and guys parading around majestically like something out of a Busby Berkeley musical. Then a girl, naked from the waist up, came out and played Bach's "Toccata and Fugue" in D minor on the accordion. Afterward, we compared notes.

"Did you get a hard-on?"

"No, I didn't get a hard-on. Did you get a hard-on?"

"No, I didn't get a hard-on. Not even close."

Johnny summed it up perfectly: "That J.S. Bach. What a hard-on-killer!"

We all cracked up. It was so un-sexy. I guess the whole thing was cooked up for the American tourists who shock so easily.

The next day and the day after that, we toured around Paris in the bus, taking in all the mandatory sights: The Champs Élysées, the Eifel Tower, the Louvre, the Rodin Museum, the Seine, and some of the cafes on the Left Bank, including the famous Deux Maggots, which turned out to be an overpriced tourist trap. At one stop, I found a payphone and tried to call Martisse. But a concierge answered and told me she was not there. She was the lifeline I was hoping for, but now it looked like I might be on my own. Tomorrow, the bus would leave for Holland, KLM, America—without me.

III

I had already made a checklist: 1) Write letter to parents: "Dear Mom and Dad, Sorry to alarm you, but I must do this. Don't worry about me; I will be alright…" 2) Write note to Art: "Dear Art, I know this will cause you a lot of trouble and worry. I'm sorry, but I must stay here. Please don't try to look for me or call the cops. I will be alright…" 3) Write note to Robin "Dear Robin, I lied when I said I was being faithful to someone back home. There's no one back home. It was because of this. I couldn't tell anyone I was planning to escape into Paris. I have never met anyone I've wanted to be with more than you. I wish you could escape with me, but you have a great future at Cooper Union, and I wouldn't want to mess that up. I don't know what will become of me, but I can only hope that someday we will meet again. Love, Eddie." 4) Go to American Express and cash in all traveler's checks.

I knew they could trace me from my visit to American Express, so I had to go there only once and then disappear. My parents had given me $100 in traveler's checks to cover my sundry expenses. This, plus the $500 from my grandfather's coin collection, made it $600. I had already cashed in $50, so that left $550 I needed to claim before the dragnet closed in.

At about five in the morning, I silently packed my suitcase and knapsack, left the note for Art, left the note for Robin slipped under her door, and left the youth hostel. The concierge was asleep. The street was wet from the street cleaners, and I could tell the day was going to be hot. "Paris when it sizzles." This was August, and Paris had been sizzling since July. It was just getting light. I had no idea how I was going to get to the Left Bank, but I would find a way. Was the Métro running? Maybe I could get a cab…

The American Express at Montmartre was closed. I would have to wait until it opened to get my dough, and it would be better to stay in this area so no one could trace me to the Left Bank. I tried Martisse again. A male voice answered, gruffly annoyed at having been woken up at this hour. I asked for Martisse, and he rang through to her room. No answer. At five o'clock in the morning, this really worried me. She was my only native contact in Paris. What had become of her? I was worried, not only for myself, but for her.

I climbed the many steps, through the beautiful park on the hillside, toward the basilica. I thought about the chaos that would soon be reigning at the youth hostel when they discovered I was gone. When I reached the top tier, I looked out over the whole of Paris. The early morning light came streaming down, giving Paris the aura of a heavenly city. It was a transcendental moment for me. I knew this place was my destiny. If I never saw New York again, that was okay by me. Anyway, that's how I felt at that moment.

I went back down into the park and sat under a tree. I hoped no one would come up here looking for me. I had to kill almost three hours. I sat with my back to the tree, facing uninhabited shrubbery, hoping no one would notice me. I'd started writing in a spiral notebook. It was a sort of journal, what I hoped might become my first book; *Paris Memoirs*, I would call it—unless I thought of something better.

At eight o'clock, I was in front of the American Express office when they opened up. I signed all my traveler's checks, showed my passport, and was given 3,185 francs, mostly in 100-franc notes. I split it into two stacks and stuck a stack of bills in each sock. I was now very vulnerable to theft, with no safe place to stash the dough. I kept a few smaller bills in my pockets for food and carfare. I grabbed a map of the métro and a Paris street map. After puzzling over how I would get to Martisse's address, which was on rue des Fossés Saint-Jacques, right near the Sorbonne, I saw there was no fast and simple way I could get there with the métro, so I decided to take a cab. I asked the American Express lady where the nearest place I could get a taxi was, and she directed me to rue Caulaincourt a few blocks west.

The morning rush hour had begun, and the taxi crawled through dense traffic. We crossed the Seine to the Left Bank. Rue des Fossés Saint-Jacques was a narrow, curving street off rue Saint-Jacques. The building was old and run-down, yellowish with shutters. On the ground floor was a bookstore. I approached the concierge, a tiny, wrinkled woman in her sixties with dyed blonde hair, meticulously made-up with lipstick, rouge, and false eyelashes. She was dressed to the nines in a magenta tailored suit that looked like it could've come from Dior or something and a saucy little magenta béret, tilted just so. I asked her in very polite French if Mlle Verneuil was at home.

"She just arrived an hour ago," the old lady said. I was delighted and relieved. "She was very tired. She's sleeping now. Why don't you come back this afternoon?"

"Alright, thank you, Madame," I said.

"You're welcome." She gave me a coquettish smile.

I walked up to the Sorbonne campus, which was mostly deserted, then over to the Boulevard Saint-Michel ("Boul'Miche," the locals called it). This was where all the cool cafés were. I immediately spotted the Café Dupont. Lots of tables out front and more inside. By now it was about ten a.m., and I was very tired and hungry. The suitcase, sleeping bag, and knapsack I was toting were getting quite heavy. The breakfast crowd was trickling in. This looked to be a student hangout. I grabbed a table, flagged down a waiter, and ordered café au lait, a croissant, and two eggs. I didn't know how to say sunnyside up or over easy, so when the waiter asked me "Brouillés?", I said "Oui." I soon found out it meant scrambled. At this point, anything in my stomach would be welcome. It might have been the best meal I ever had; the strong, hot coffee, the croissant with that wonderful butter they have, and the eggs—not too hard, not runny—just perfect. Simple, yet perfect. Yes, the French certainly know their food.

I was feeling much better now. The food in my stomach and the fact that Martisse was there went a long way to calming my nerves, although I knew the cops would soon be out in force, searching for me. I wondered if I could find someone to forge me a new passport with a fake name. Meanwhile, I kept on the new, hip shades I'd recently purchased. They were the kind with curved plastic lenses fastened to just a single metal strip on top. Anyway, they obscured enough of my face to make it hard for the cops to recognize me.

As I listened to the conversations surrounding me, I gradually realized I was hearing no French. There was German, English, Italian, various African languages, maybe Arabic. Looking at them, I guessed many of these must be Sorbonne students from other countries. Then I remembered: The French all flee Paris in August. They were all on the Côte, where I had just come from, or one of the Atlantic beaches, like Biarritz. I was just another tourist in a sea of tourists.

I sat in the café until one o'clock, when everything closes. Then I wandered the deserted streets, with my luggage growing ever heavier, and looked in store windows. I needed to pee. At length, I realized that these metal-partitioned things on the street were *pissoirs*. I entered the next one I saw. There were foot-shaped metal plates where you were supposed to place your feet, so I did. And I peed, breathing through my mouth against the smell. I wanted Martisse to get her rest, so I waited until three, then headed back to her place.

This time, the bench in the lobby was occupied by two shady-looking characters: A very big guy with very short hair and a smaller, wiry guy with a black beard who looked kind of like an Arab. They gave me the fisheye.

The concierge smiled. "Je suis désolé, monsieur, mais Mlle Verneuil does not wish to be disturbed. You are the américain boy from Saint-Tropez, no?" There was something fishy about this concierge, too nice, too solicitous—in a phony way.

"Yes," I said. *So Martisse told her about me.*

"She asks that you meet her at Café le Sélect at six this evening."

"Et où est ce café?"

"99 Boulevard du Montparnasse."

"Très bien," I said, crestfallen, and left.

Now what was I to do? I trudged, bag and baggage, to the nearby Luxembourg Gardens. I was thoroughly worn out. I sat on a bench and just thought. I wondered if Martisse would keep giving me the runaround. I wondered if I had made a mistake taking off like this. I thought about my friends leaving for home without me and how they must feel. I thought about Robin. I thought about my parents and hoped they weren't having a nervous breakdown. I felt sad, and a little scared. I looked at my watch. Four o'clock. I decided to head over to the Sélect. I studied my map. It was only about a ten-minute walk.

The first things that hit me were the smells. An odd mixture of apples, smoke, garlic, and human sweat. I had already noticed that Europeans generally did not wear deodorant. It was a big room, with more tables on the sidewalk. There was a bar, several long tables for large parties, and many small tables. I took one of these. Lots of waiters scurried back and forth. Eventually, one took my order: "Vin rouge." The place was beginning to fill up after *sieste*. I read my book and nursed my wine.

Suddenly, there was a guy at my table. "You like that book?" He was American, and he was talking about *Cool City*, which I had been reading little bits at a time since the trip began.

"Yeah. You know this book?"

"You could say that. I wrote it."

I looked up in amazement. Before me sat a short, middle-aged man. Receding dark hair, thick-framed glasses. "*You're* Nick duMornay?"

"C'est moi, mon vieux."

"Oh my God! What are the odds?" Then I started babbling on about his character, Danny, and how much I identified with him, and how so many of the kids I knew in New York were reading this book. He was obviously basking in this outpouring of admiration.

"And who might you be, young man?" I told him my name and—perhaps unwisely—about my escapade. He got a good laugh out of my story. "So, this Martisse is supposed to meet you here at six?"

"Yes."

Apparently, my voice betrayed my trepidation because he said, "Well if she doesn't show up, you can crash at my place."

"Really? That's so kind. You live near here?"

"Pretty near."

"Thank you. That's really nice of you!"

"One thing I ask in exchange: You let me steal your story for my next book."

"Well…see…I don't want to seem ungrateful, but I'm a writer too, and I was kinda planning to write this one myself. In fact, I *am* writing it." I showed him my spiral notebook.

"Ah, a kindred spirit! Well, no matter. The offer still stands. Stories are as plentiful as stars. Perhaps I can help you in some way."

"Wow! Thanks, Nick!"

"Call me Irving."

"Irving?"

"Yes, Irving Moskowitz. That's my real name. Nick duMornay is my *nom de plume.*"

Irving Moskowitz? The Jews are dogging my steps! "Okay. Thanks, Irving!"

We ordered more wine, and I paid. It occurred to me that he might be an imposter, but his intimate knowledge of all the details of *Cool City* assuaged my suspicions. He was the real article alright. Irving held forth on life, New York, Paris, and writing. I guess he was pretty fond of hearing himself talk, and I was only too happy to listen. I looked at my watch. Six thirty-five, and still no Martisse. I spotted a payphone and decided to call her. As I was dialing, she walked in.

It was a shock. She wore a short, low-cut dress that revealed her spectacular body in excruciating detail. She wore loads of makeup, and frankly, she looked—slutty! I quickly hung up the phone and waved so she would see me. I walked to the table where Irving sat. She met me there and hugged and kissed me on both cheeks. I felt my face go all hot and red.

"Martisse, this is Irving. He wrote this book!" I held up the book, smiling idiotically.

Irving kissed her hand. "Enchanté, Mademoiselle." Then to me: "Elle est très charmant!"

"Did you really wrote this?" Martisse said in her cute broken English. Irving nodded. "But eet says 'Neek duMornay.'"

Irving explained about the nom de plume. Then, "Well, I really must be toddling off. I have an appointment in Saint-Germain. Eddie, you have my address. Stay in touch!" We shook hands, and he was off.

Alone at last with Martisse. I didn't comment on her appearance, but I wondered about it. "I…thought I'd never see you," I said, searching for something to say. There was something about her eyes that was distant, foggy. "Are you alright?"

"Oh, yes. I'm fine," she said.

"You came in so late, and you slept so late. I was worried."

"Ah well, we keep strange hours here in Paris."

"Can I buy you dinner?"

"If you are eating, I will eat also."

I ordered dinner for both of us. Le Sélect was not known for their cuisine, but Irving had told me they served a great eggplant dish called *aubergine*, a staple among the poor and threadbare on the Left Bank. It had potatoes in it, and it was very filling. Just what I needed right now; I was starting to get that starving artist look already.

"Do you know of a place I can rent a room cheap?" I said.

"Perhaps Mme La Brot, my landlady, will know of something for you. I will ask her tonight."

She was talking about the sleazy concierge in the bright pink getup. "Can I go with you and ask her after dinner?"

"Non…is better if I talk to her alone."

We had a few more glasses of wine during and after dinner. It was starting to go to my head. "But *please* can't I go with you now?" I was beginning to slur my words. "I'm getting *very tired*."

"Non. I have…I have to work."

"Work? What work are you doing dressed like that?" I really didn't want a truthful answer to that, but I got it.

"'Night work.' I have to go now. Thank you for the dinner. You call me later, yes?"

I suddenly got very sober. "'Night work'?"

"I have to go. Call me at three."

"In the morning?"

"Oui."

"But I'll never stay awake that long! *Très fatigué!*"

"Voila." She fished in her purse and placed a small blue pill on the table before me, got up, and walked out as fast as her spike-heeled pumps could carry her.

I downed the pill with some wine and just sat there, staring at the invisible trail of perfume in her wake.

Behind me, I heard voices. There was a group of young people, mostly guys, but I heard one or two female voices, and they were speaking English. Suddenly I felt completely awake, alive, and confident. I turned and saw the motley crew gathered at the long table behind me. There were four guys and two girls, all in their twenties. Most sounded American, but I heard a British and I think a Swedish accent in there. They were dressed in various degrees of arty-casual. From the paint-spattered overalls and T-shirts, I deduced that some were artists. One guy had wild hair, glasses, and a corduroy blazer. I pegged him as a writer. The girls were dressed mostly in black and reminded me of beatnik chicks I had seen in Greenwich Village. They were acting all cool and sophisticated, but I could see at once they were poseurs. They were having some kind of debate about Sartre and Camus. Which one was the true existentialist? Or maybe neither. My senses were vibrating with energy, blasting information into my brain. Wow! What was in that pill? Some kind of speed, I surmised. One thing for sure, I wasn't tired anymore. I decided to address the assembled multitudes.

"Existentialism is bullshit!" I proclaimed. I had tried to read *No Exit* by Sartre and *The Stranger* by Camus, but I couldn't get through either of them. They just bored the hell out of me. "Now, *this* guy," I held up *Cool City* by Nick duMornay, "*this* guy's got the answers!" They all howled with laughter.

"You mean *Irving*?" said the writer-looking guy. I guessed Irving was pretty much a fixture around here.

"Yeah."

"Irving couldn't write his way out of a paper bag."

"Well," said I, "I beg to differ."

"He begs to differ," the writer guy said in a mocking tone. They all guffawed some more.

"Writing should entertain, first and foremost. Sartre and Camus are *not* entertaining, and Irving is."

"Well," said the Swedish painter, "not all writing must entertain. Some writing enlightens."

"Well, if it enlightens and doesn't entertain, I've got no use for it."

Then one of the girls—she was blonde and quite pretty—chimed in. "Maybe when you're older, young man, you'll acquire a taste for real literature." She had her hair bobbed short, like Jean Seberg in *Breathless*. In fact, she looked quite a lot like Jean Seberg. That movie had been a big influence on me and my decision to live in Paris.

What a condescending bitch, I thought, *but she's hot.* "Thanks for the words of wisdom, Grandma," I said. "What're you, twenty?"

"Twenty-one."

Just then, Charlie Parker came on the jukebox. It was Diz & Bird doing "Au Privave." I knew every note. I started scat singing to it, playing an invisible saxophone and dancing around like a crazy person. When the record ended, they all laughed and clapped. That's when I decided they were alright. "Hey, kid," said a tall, sallow guy with long, stringy hair, wearing a white, short-sleeved shirt and brown baggy pants, "how'd you like to come to a party with us?"

I was surprised at this sudden friendliness. "I'd love to, but I've gotta look after all my stuff." I indicated my suitcase and knapsack, which had my sleeping bag tied to the top.

"That's alright," said Brian the Brit, who had fair, curly hair and blue eyes, "I'll speak to Jacques, the proprietor. He'll keep your stuff safe. Nobody'll steal it from the back room."

"What if they do?" I said. "Will you pay for it?"

"I will. The last thing this place wants is the cops showing up."

That was the last thing I wanted too. "Okay, speak to Jacques. Is the party close by?"

"Very."

I stashed my stuff in Jacques' back room, and we were off. It was literally just around the corner. 48 rue Vavin was another yellowish building with shutters (there were a lot of those on the *rive gauche*). It had tall French windows and a double door painted green. Up two flights, and we were at the front door of chez Alexandre something. I didn't catch the last name. Alexandre was actually French. He gave us a boisterous welcome and ushered us into the cavernous living room, handing each of us a glass of wine in a paper cup. Even with its high ceiling and chandelier, the place was thick with Gaulois smoke and the buzz of animated conversation in French and English. There were at least forty people gathered in the big living room and adjoining kitchen, mostly arty student-types in their twenties. There was a big cast iron pan on the stove containing—guess what—*aubergine*. People were serving themselves and eating out of various dishes and bowls. Even if I hadn't just eaten this very dish, food would've been the last thing on my mind. That pill had wiped out any trace of an appetite. But I certainly was rattling on like an idiot.

Almost everyone spoke both French and English. On the way over, we had all still been talking about existentialism. "It's such a depressing philosophy," I was saying. "The main thrust of it seems to be 'life has no point, and there's no reason for living,' which might be true, but why dwell on it?"

"Life is short, talk is cheap, so let's all drink and fuck and eat!" said Jean-Marc, the writerly-looking guy in the corduroy jacket. Everyone had a good laugh at that.

"Hey, that's good!" I said. "Original?"

"Yeah."

I hadn't noticed his French accent before; his English was quite perfect. "Man, I wish I could speak French like you speak English."

"My mother is American; my father is French."

At the far end of the room was a grand piano, and soon a group of jazz musicians began to play "Willow Weep for Me." There was a tenor sax, piano, bass, and drums. *Damn! That tenor player is good. Hmmm, he sounds familiar...* I worked my way through the crowd until I could see... *My god! That's Dexter Gordon...and Bud Powell...and Kenny Clarke...* There was a white guy on bass I didn't recognize, but he was also world class. This was a jazz hippie's wet dream come true. I started swaying and moving around to the beautiful ballad. I just wanted to sit down and listen, but the speed wouldn't let me. I had my eyes closed, and soon there was someone in my arms. I found myself slow-dancing with Charlotte, the blonde American girl who'd given me such a hard time at the Sélect.

"Oh. Hello. What're you doing here?"

"Dancing with you." She smiled up at me. She was quite petite.

These Paris Americans were certainly changeable. I pointed out that we were dancing to none other than Dexter Gordon. She hadn't heard of him. I then proceeded to run off at the mouth for about fifteen minutes on Dexter, Bud, Kenny, and all the giants of jazz I had heard and seen in New York. I was quite the chatterbox on this drug. "Where are you from?" I asked her.

"Stockbridge, Massachusetts. It's a small town, but it's really nice."

"Why are you suddenly so really nice?" I asked.

"I don't know. I guess I'm sorry I was mean to you before."

"Oh, that's alright. I was acting like quite a jerk myself. See, this girl gave me a pill so I could stay awake, and boy, did it work."

"I *see*," she said as if this cleared up a lot of things for her. "You know, of course, that that girl is a prostitute."

"Yeah, I know. So, are you an artist?" I said, adroitly changing the subject.

"I'm an actress."

"I *see*," I said, kind of pulling her leg.

"I'm going to be in a play at the American Theater. *Hedda Gabler*. I play Hedda!"

"No kidding? That's terrific. You must be awfully good."

"Yes, I am. It's my calling."

"Can I go?"

"Of course. We're in rehearsals right now, but it opens Friday. I'll get you a ticket."

Boy, I didn't know what had come over me. I was turning into a real Don Juan.

Dexter and the band started into "Our Love Is Here to Stay," a slightly more uptempo piece. Without warning, Charlotte flew off onto the dance floor, where some space had now appeared, and launched into a beautifully choreographed, almost balletic dance. I hadn't noticed before, but she was wearing a black one-piece leotard and plaid sarong skirt. Now she shed the sarong, kicked off her shoes, and launched into some very impressive twirls and gymnastic dance moves. The onlookers gave her room to do her thing, and Charlotte twirled and swooped to the music. Afterward, everyone applauded and Charlotte soaked it up.

"Wow, Charlotte. You sure do have talent."

"I know. I can't really take credit," she said. "Some people are just born with it."

Charlotte and I talked a long time. She mostly talked about herself and her aspirations. We listened to Dexter, and after his set, we walked up and introduced ourselves, and I gushed about what a big fan I was. He was very friendly. I also shook hands with Bud Powell and Kenny Clarke and told them what a big fan I was. The speed was making me feel a bit too edgy, so I had a couple more drinks: A Pernaud and a brandy. That definitely took the edge off.

"Well," I said to Charlotte, "I have to leave soon, but I'd sure like to see you again."

"You will. On Friday. Remember?" She wrote her phone number and address on a paper napkin and gave it to me. "Call me and I'll arrange to leave your ticket at the box office." Then, "You're meeting that prostitute, aren't you?"

"Yes. She said she'd help me find a place to stay. Besides, she's a very nice girl, no matter what."

"I can give you a place to stay. At least for tonight."

"Really?"

"Yes. Meg and I have a very nice apartment, and you can have the couch."

"I appreciate the offer, but Martisse is expecting me…"

"Oh yes, with bated breath, I'm sure."

I decided she was just a shade too snotty, and besides, I was still terribly curious about Martisse.

"What time does the Sélect close?"

"I'm not sure. Hey, Meg," she called to her friend, "what time does le Sélect close?"

"Three a.m."

"I'd better get over there and get my stuff. Can I have a raincheck on your offer?"

"Oh sure. We're open all night, every night."

Definitely too snotty.

I shook hands with Charlotte, Meg and all the guys from the Sélect and our host, Alexandre, and then I walked back to the Sélect. Jacques, a big, jovial character, showed me where my stuff was.

"Bon chance, mon petit," he said as I picked up my things and started walking toward Martisse's place.

I got there well before three. I didn't feel like hanging around, talking to Mme LaBrot—she gave me the creeps—so I just hung out on the street outside her building, where I could see her coming when she came. I waited about half an hour. It gradually occurred to me that maybe she was already in her apartment. So, I went inside. Of course, Mme LaBrot was not at the desk at this hour. One of the thuggish-looking guys—the big one with the crewcut—was dozing, with his head on the desk.

"Ahem!" His head popped up. He regarded me contemptuously. "Mlle Verneuil, est elle ici?"

"Oui, mais elle est occupé." He gave me a malicious smile.

My heart sank. I knew what he meant by "occupé." She was entertaining a gentleman caller, to put it delicately. The thug behind the desk asked me if I wanted to wait. I nodded my head.

"Asseyez-vous la." He indicated the bench against the left wall of the lobby. I sat down listlessly. The minutes crawled by. I took out my journal and began to write. This new, sad turn in my real-life story prompted a parallel turn in my made-up story.

While I waited, several ladies of the evening paraded through the lobby with clients in tow and took the elevator up. After about thirty minutes, I heard the creak of the elevator coming down. It was an aged contraption, the old-fashioned kind in a shaft made of filigreed iron with the stairs winding around it. A man, middle-aged with tortoiseshell eyeglasses and lightweight sports coat, emerged from the elevator and, eyes to the ground, moved quickly past me and out the front door.

The desk thug sleepily plugged a jack into the switchboard and picked up the receiver. "Ce garçon américain est ici." He nodded, then hung up and pointed to the elevator. "Deuxième étage, numero 204." It only being one flight up, I opted for the stairs.

Martisse opened the door wearing nothing but a man's dress shirt; her makeup was smeared, and her hair was in disarray.

"Am I intruding?"

"Non. What time is it?"

I looked at my watch. "Three forty-five." She stepped back to let me in. The place was just one, big, messy room. She was not exactly a fastidious little homemaker. It smelled of paint and turpentine, and she had a professional easel set up near the tall window. There were some paintings on the wall I figured were hers. Semi-professional. I actually thought they were pretty good. "Well, I guess it's too late to talk to Mme LaBrot about a room for me."

"Oui. She never works this late."

"Then, why did you…" I stopped myself. "Can I crash on your floor? Just for tonight?"

"You can cresh on my bed if you like. Excuse me. I haf to make myself clean."

That'll take some doing, I thought.

She took some things (I couldn't see what) out of the top drawer of her dresser, went down the hall to the bathroom, and left me sitting on her unmade bed, which smelled of sex.

I was very uncomfortable and filled with bitterness and foreboding. She must've been in the loo for fifteen minutes. Finally, she returned, staggering a bit, and sat on the bed beside me. Her hair was wet, her makeup all washed off, and she smelled fresh and soapy. She still wore nothing but the big shirt. My heart was pounding. I couldn't help it; every time she got near me, my heart went crazy. She had something in her right hand; I couldn't see what it was.

"Want some heroin?" Then I saw she had a syringe in her hand. "I'll do it for you. It feels great."

"N-no. I've never done anything stronger than pot. Won't I get addicted? Are *you* addicted?"

A long pause as her head drooped down and sort of bobbed up and down. "Oui…but you won't get hooked from just once."

"No, thanks." I was impressed with how quickly her English was improving.

"Okay. You can sleep in the bed. With me. Okay?"

"Uh, yeah."

She unbuttoned her shirt, and there it was: the Garden of Eden. She got under the sheet and beckoned me inside. Even though I now knew for sure that she was both a junkie and a hooker, I couldn't stop myself. I wanted her on some kind of insane, primal level. I got undressed as fast as I could, and then…

As I mentioned earlier, I had gone all the way twice before. But it was never any good. But now, with Martisse, it was. Boy, *was* it. This was the greatest experience of my life up to this point. I was hooked alright, but not on drugs. On her.

"Martisse, je t'aime," I said afterward. "Je t'aime toujours." She had passed out.

In retrospect, I kinda doubt it was very Earth-shattering for her. I mean, do prostitutes even enjoy sex? She made a lot of noise when we were doing it, which made me think she was enjoying it, but in retrospect, I think she was probably faking it.

When we awoke sometime in the afternoon, I was troubled but still in love with her. "Come," I said, "I'll buy you breakfast—or lunch, or whatever this is."

"Okay."

Under Mme LaBrot's watchful gaze, we passed through the lobby and went to a small bistro nearby and had croissants and café au lait. She had made herself beautiful again.

Over coffee, she fixed me with a serious look. "I need you to help me with something. It is very important," she said.

"What?"

"Come with me to Marseille. I need to score some sheet and bring it back to Paris. You will make us look innocent."

"Innocent to whom?"

"The cops, of course."

So, this was her master plan. Her reason for sleeping with me. Her reason for befriending me in Saint-Tropez in the first place. "Martisse, I need to tell you something."

"What?"

"The cops are looking for *me*. I sneaked out of the youth hostel and ran away. I'm not going back to America with the camp group. I'm sure they've called the cops by now."

"Oh, merde! That ruins everything."

"Well...there *might* be a way..."

"What?"

"Do you know someone who can make me a false passport?"

She thought about this for a while. "Peut-être."

"If you do this for me, I'll make the trip with you."

"I will have to ask Mme LaBrot."

"What's Mme LaBrot got to do with this?"

"She is in charge."

"Hmm, I thought it was something like that."

"This will cost a lot. Probably 5,000."

"Then that would be my payment for making the trip."

"I was going to share the profits with you."

"I don't want that kind of money," I said "Anyway, I haven't got that much, so she would have to put it up, or I can't go."

She smiled. "You are not as innocent as you look, mon petit chou-chou. Okay, allons-y!" She yanked me by the arm, and off we went to see Mme LaBrot.

Mme LaBrot was still lurking behind the concierge desk. When Martisse asked for a private audience, she led us through an unmarked door and into a well-appointed apartment. When she heard my request, she looked at me with a mixture of amusement and disdain. She and Martisse had an animated conversation in French. Most of it was too fast for me to catch, but the gist was that LaBrot didn't want to lay out the bread and Martisse was fighting for me. At last, she relented. She went to her safe, extracted a wad of cash, which she gave to Martisse, along with an address. She said we should go see a guy named André.

"I need a disguise," I said in the taxi. "How about a false beard and mustache?"

"Mais, non! You must look innocent."

"The cops will have a picture of me, so I must have some kind of disguise. How about glasses?"

"What's wrong with the sunglasses you are wearing?"

"No, for the passport picture. You can't wear sunglasses in those."

"Okay. We will get some glasses." She gave the cabbie some directions, and he took us to a theatrical prop shop near the American Theater, on rue de la Tombe Issoire. There, I found a perfect pair of black-rimmed prop glasses I could see through without the distortion of a prescription. Martisse laughed when I put them on. I guess I looked pretty silly.

Now we rode all across Paris into a remote industrial neighborhood where everything was drab and gray to a small redbrick building sandwiched between a garage and some kind of factory.

"Attendez ici," Martisse told the cabbie. She knocked three times, then two more on the unmarked wooden door. A peephole scrutinized us, then the door opened and André, a small bald man of sixty, let us in. He peered at us over his spectacles.

"Martisse?"

"Oui."

Martisse introduced me and filled him in on what we wanted. He asked me what kind of passport I wanted.

"De quel pays?" (From what country?)

"British—uh, d'Angleterre," I said without hesitation. I had thought this all through. I didn't want an American one, because the cops would be looking for a kid with an American passport, but since I obviously spoke English, I figured I could pull off British. He asked to see my U.S. passport. He carefully scrutinized all the entrance and exit stamps I had accumulated in my travels.

"You want all these?" he said in English.

"No, just leaving Great Britain and arrivé en France," I said, half in English, half in French. "Oh, and can you put a student visa stamp good for one year?"

"I can, but it's only good for six months, then you have to have it renewed."

"Okay," I said.

"Can I hold on to this?" he asked, holding up my passport. I nodded. "Now we need to take your picture," he said. I put on the glasses, and he snapped my picture with a big camera on a tripod.

"And what is your new name?" he asked me.

"Jesse Bright." And I wrote it out for him on a piece of paper. I also gave myself a fake London address and new birthday, one in which I was eighteen.

"Combien de temps?" Martisse asked him.

"Deux jours. Come back day after tomorrow."

Martisse gave him a down payment of fifty percent of his fee, and we bade him adieu.

"Why 'Jesse Bright?'" she asked as we rode back toward the Left Bank.

"My *nom de plume*," I said.

With two days to kill, I expected to have two more blissful nights in Martisse's bed. But no such luck. I didn't realize how important it was to her—and Mme LaBrot—to keep working. She needed to get her money so she could get her smack. So, Mme LaBrot gave me a small room on the top floor with a narrow bed and a scratchy blanket.

I quickly realized Mme LaBrot was running a full-fledged brothel. Behind every door in the five-story building, there lived a girl who sold her body for a living. There was Yvette, a tall blonde, Charo, a Spanish dancer, Lili, a French pastry gone a bit stale, and lots of others. Of course, none of them held a candle to Martisse, and I could see she was also Mme LaBrot's favorite. I was forbidden to disturb Martisse without calling her from the lobby. I barely saw her at all until it was time to pick up my new passport and leave for the station.

IV We arrived at the Gare de Lyon in time to catch the four o'clock train. Martisse bought our round trip tickets. While she was doing that, I did a very smart thing: I rented one of those lockers they have in train stations, and in it I stashed my suitcase with most of my money and my sleeping bag. I just packed a few clothes and my new passport in my knapsack and kept a small amount of cash in my pocket. The U.S. passport stayed in my suitcase. There was no way I was gonna leave all that stuff at Martisse's place, not with that landlady and those greasy thugs hanging around.

I went over to the newsstand and picked up a Paris edition of the *Herald-Tribune* and the two biggest Paris newspapers: *Le Monde* and *Le Parisien*. I wanted to see if any news of my disappearance had been published.

That's when I saw the cops. A couple of gendarmes were looking at a photo, then scrutinizing the passersby. A terrible feeling of dread came over me. Deep down, I knew it was me they were looking for. I acted nonchalant, strolled over to one of the wooden benches filled with people reading newspapers and magazines, and sat down. I opened *Le Parisien*, the tabloid, and started to read, looking as inconspicuous as I possibly could.

"Monsieur." I looked up. It was the two cops. They looked at their photo, looked at me, then back at the photo. "C'est lui!" said one to the other.

"Non, je ne crois pas," said the other. "Votre passport, s'il vous plait," he said to me.

I presented my forged British passport. "What's this all about?" I asked in my best indignant British accent.

He ignored me, turned to the other cop. "Voila. Ce n'est pas lui."

They turned and walked away. Martisse then rushed up to me and said, "Allons-y. Se dépechêr!" She whisked me away to the platform.

The train made several stops—at Dijon, Lyon, and Avignon — and it hung around for a while at each station, so the ride seemed to take forever. At some point, Martisse got up and went to the restroom for a long time. When she came back, I could tell she had shot up again. Then she fell asleep with her head on my shoulder. I was too nervous to fall asleep or even close my eyes. I combed through the papers, looking for my name or picture, but thankfully, I was not there. I did, however, notice a disturbing story about several prostitutes being murdered. They had dubbed the murderer "le tueur de prostituées" (the hooker killer). The killings were extremely gruesome, the victims were all stabbed multiple times in their own beds.

I wrote in my journal. I continued the unfolding story of my semi-fictional protagonist, Frankie Walz. The words came pouring out of me as if a sluice had suddenly opened in a long pent-up stream. I was no longer simply recording my European adventure, I was embroidering, adding dramatic flourishes, entertaining my imagined audience.

Outside, the French countryside whizzed by; almost the reverse of the bus trip up from the *côte*. We arrived at Gare de Marseille-Saint-Charles at around ten at night. It was almost as impressive as the Gare de Lyon, but relatively empty except for a few shady-looking loiterers that leaned on pillars and walls. Martisse left me with the bags and went off to make a phone call. A man came up to me and offered to carry our bags. There were only my knapsack and her large purse. I politely declined. He hovered near me for a few anxious moments, apparently weighing the pros and cons of stealing them from me, then he went away. After ten minutes, Martisse returned with an address scribbled on a slip of paper. We got into one of the taxis that were lined up at the curb outside.

It took us into a jumble of crooked streets and alleys called *le Panier*, Marseille's old quarter near the waterfront. We got out at a run-down building with no lights showing. Martisse rang the doorbell. After a while an eye scrutinized us through a peephole. Then a man's voice shouted gruffly, "Qui est?"

"Martisse de Mme LaBrot."

The door opened, and a large unsmiling man in a sweaty undershirt and workman's cap let us in. He had a week's growth of beard, and he smelled. I'd gotten used to everyone stinking of sweat and garlic by now, but this guy was a standout. The large, dirty apartment had unvarnished wood floors and shabby furniture.

"Viens," he said, and we followed him down a dark corridor with closed doors on either side and into a large office with an oriental rug on the floor and polished wooden desk. Behind the desk sat a dark, fat man with tinted black-framed glasses that made his eyes look freakishly large. Martisse held out her hand to shake his, but out of nowhere, two men—the guy who ushered us in and another thug—grabbed us, threw us down onto a couch opposite the desk, and proceeded to rifle through our bags. They found the drug money in Martisse's purse—24,000 francs—and gave it to their boss. They also took her drug stash.

"Hey!" Martisse yelled. "What do you think you're doing?"

"We are robbing you, mademoiselle," the fat man said casually.

"Who the hell are you anyway? Where is Labay? We have an arrangement."

"Labay is dead. We have taken over his operation. I am Mariani."

"When Mme LaBrot finds out about this, she'll have your head! We came to buy, not be robbed!"

With a slight gesture of his head, Mariani had his thugs tie our hands behind our backs and gag us with filthy rags. Then they threw us into a large closet with a dusty, splintery floor and locked us in. A bare light bulb glared at us from the ceiling. The space was empty except for us. We could hear them talking in Mariani's office, just outside the door. They were debating what to do with us. I didn't catch all the Corsican slang, but the gist of it, it seemed to me, was that they had to make us "disappear." There was only one way to interpret that, and I was scared shitless.

"We will need a boat," said Mariani. "Where is Manazzu?"

"At sea, fishing," answered the thug who had let us in.

"Well, when will he back? We need to dispose of the bodies at sea."

"Tomorrow. Day after, the latest."

Martisse and I looked at each other, wide-eyed, as we slid down to the floor with our backs against the wall.

After a while, I closed my eyes and tried to get some rest. Sleep was out of the question, but my body needed rest. I don't know how much time went by. I must have dozed off, because I was awakened by desperate noises from Martisse. I looked over and saw her sweating profusely and shivering. Her skin was a ghastly shade of white. She was uttering imploring sounds through her gag. Gradually, I realized she was going through withdrawals. She was in agony. I wanted desperately to help her, but what could I do? I started working on the ropes behind my back. If I kept tugging, I was sure I could eventually wriggle my hands free. Just then, I heard a key turn in the lock. The big lug who had greeted us at the door entered with a tray of food. He untied our hands and gags to let us eat the bread, cheese, and tea. No utensils were provided. As soon as her gag was off, Martisse told him in a frenzied stream of words I barely understood that she was "jonesing" and he had to get her a shot or she would die. His response was the equivalent of "tough shit." He got up and left us there with our food.

"Non, *non!*" Martisse cried after him. The door slammed and locked and she broke down crying.

"Martisse, do you have any hairpins in your hair?" I noticed her hair was pulled back and up in what they call a French Twist. She pulled out a hairpin and gave it to me. Her hand was shaking so badly, I had trouble grabbing it. "Please, try to hang on. I'm going to get us out of here. With this." I put the hairpin in my shirt pocket. I thought back to my criminal past in New York and how I impressed the JDs by breaking into that garbage truck.

I ate all the bread and cheese. Martisse said she couldn't eat. I made her drink some tea, but she threw it up after only a few minutes. Before long, the two thugs returned. "Toilette, toilette!" we implored. While his buddy watched me, the big guy walked Martisse to the bathroom. Then he brought her back and took me. He made me go with the door open. Then they re-tied our hands, gagged us, and left with the tray.

Again, I commenced the tugging and wrist-wriggling behind my back. Hours passed; how many, I couldn't say. At last, I got my hands free. I freed

Martisse's hands and took her gag off. She was now in a fetal position on the floor, hugging her knees, groaning softly. I made her keep quiet for some minutes so I could make sure no one was moving in the house. The creaky plank floors in this old place amplified every footstep, but now it was very quiet. If they were still out there, everyone was asleep.

I went to work on the door lock. I unbent the hairpin so it was a long, straight piece. Then I bent it into a hook shape. I felt around inside the keyhole, but I couldn't get a sense of how the mechanism worked. I decided I needed a second hairpin. I had seen people pick locks in the movies and on TV, and they always used two implements. So, I took another hairpin out of her hair and bent it in the same way as the first one. Now, I felt I was getting somewhere. After a while, I was able to turn the lock the way a key would. It gave a reassuring clunk and we were free.

I put my finger to my lips, motioning for Martisse to be very quiet. I wanted to turn off the light, but there was no light switch inside our closet. I figured it must be outside the door. I opened the door just a crack and felt around until I found the switch. I turned off the light and plunged us into total darkness. After our eyes adjusted to the darkness, I opened the door, which creaked loudly. It was as dark outside in the office as it was in our closet. No one was around.

"Come on," I whispered, "we're going to crawl out of here." Martisse grabbed on to my belt, and we started crawling through the darkness on our hands and knees. We went past several rooms that were marked by closed doors on either side of the long hallway. I thought I could hear snoring in one of them. Just then, a board creaked loudly. "Eh? Qui est la?" It was the big guy's voice. We froze, expecting to be discovered and thrown back into our closet. There was a brief silence, then, more snoring. We moved forward slowly, carefully, until we reached the front door. I stood up, unlocked the several locks, and opened the door. Then I hauled Martisse to her feet and ran into the darkened street, dragging her behind me. She paused to throw up some more liquid, then we kept running.

At the end of the block, I turned to her. "Which way?"

"À droite!"

We turned to the right and ran up the damp, cobbled street. Around the next corner, there was a bar—and it appeared to be open. It was a dark, dreary joint. Two drunks sat at small tables, passed out with their heads on their arms. Other than that, no customers. The proprietor, a crusty old character, eyed us suspiciously. I whispered to Martisse, "We have no money. What can we do?"

"I must call Mme LaBrot. Only she can get us out of here."

"Pull yourself together and get him to let you use the phone."

She took a deep breath, put her shoulders back, and walked confidently up to the old guy behind the bar. She told him we had been mugged, that we had no money. He offered to call the police. "Non," she said. "Let me call Paris. I'll reverse the charges." He gave her the phone. She had the night man wake Mme LaBrot. I heard a desperate cascade of words from Martisse, then, "Très bien. Nous attenderon à la gare" (We'll wait at the station). And she hung up. She thanked the old man profusely, took my hand, and we walked out onto the dark, wet streets.

Twenty minutes later, we reached the Gare de Marseille-Saint-Charles. On the way, Martisse, who was still shaking and sweating, explained to me that Albert (the hulking crewcut guy) and Aziz (the skinny Arabic guy), Mme LaBrot's two henchmen, were coming to get us.

"What time does their train arrive?"

"Eight o'clock."

"In the morning?"

"Oui."

We spent a long tough night huddled on a waiting room bench in the damp, deserted station. Several times, she got up to use the bathroom. I've got to hand it to Martisse. She was suffering terribly, but she suffered well. She kept her composure and never complained. Every once in a while, a gendarme would pass and give us the eye. I always averted my face, and he didn't bother us.

"What about our stuff?" I asked her. "Our passports, all that money, my *journal*?"

"Don't worry," she said. "Albert and Aziz will get everything back for us."

But I *was* worried. Now I was worried I was going to witness a bloodbath. I didn't ask any more questions. What would be the point?

Albert and Aziz got off the 8:10 from Paris, looking pissed off. Getting yanked out of bed by Mme LaBrot in the middle of the night couldn't have helped their dispositions much. Martisse and I were on the platform when the train pulled in. They brushed past us without even saying hello. We just stood there for a moment, looking at their backs. Then Albert stopped and turned around. "Well. Come on!" he said impatiently.

They said it was too early to go yet. They wanted to be sure Mariani was there when we arrived. We went and had breakfast. The two guys and I had eggs and ham. Martisse just had coffee, and she was able to keep it down.

Albert regarded her. "You look terrible," he said.

"Leave her alone," I said, with an assertiveness that surprised me. And he did.

At nine, we grabbed a taxi in front of the station, and Martisse gave Mariani's address. They had the cabbie park up the street a few dozen yards and wait. They made us go with them to the front door and stand there, where we could be seen through the peephole, while Albert and Aziz crouched on either side. They each pulled out a large automatic pistol. With great trepidation, I rang the bell.

"Knock. Loud," said Albert.

I knocked loud. A familiar eye appeared at the peephole and bugged out when he saw us standing there. Apparently a little light on brains, he yanked the door open without thinking. As soon as he did, Albert and Aziz had a gun to each of his temples.

"Aren't you going to invite us in?" said Albert.

"Entrez." And he stepped back to let us.

Martisse glared at him. "Cochon!" she muttered and spat in his face.

Aziz frisked the guy and took a large switchblade knife off him.

"Take us to Mariani," Albert commanded.

He led us down the hall. Albert and Aziz shoved him, and he stumbled into Mariani's office ahead of them. Albert trained his weapon on Mariani, while Aziz came around behind the desk, frisked Mariani, and took a pistol from the top drawer.

"Give us what you took from them," said Albert, indicating me and Martisse.

"Okay, okay," said Mariani, smiling nervously. "Sois calme."

"There's one more guy around here somewhere," I chimed in.

"Call him," Albert told Mariani.

"Gasparu!" Mariani shouted. Gasparu came from one of the other rooms, raised his hands as soon as he saw what was going on.

Mariani told him to go and get our stuff. Aziz followed close behind with his gun on him. A moment later, they were back, bearing our bags and the envelope containing the money for the drugs. He dropped everything at our feet.

"What about my pocket money?" I said.

The big, stinky one reached into his pocket and plunked my few francs down on the desk.

"Now, go get us *le camelot*," said Albert.

I looked at Martisse quizzically. "It's slang for smack," she whispered.

Gasparu looked at Mariani, who gave a slight nod. Again Gasparu trudged off, with Aziz right behind him. They came back with two kilos of heroin, wrapped in plastic and brown paper.

There was a furious exchange, only some of which I got, between Mariani and Albert.

Mariani: "So now you're going to rob *us*?"

Albert: "Why not? You did it to us."

"Donnez moi un feex!" cried Martisse, desperation in her voice.

"Not now. We don't have time," said Albert.

"I *need* it!"

Then, with lightning speed, Aziz snapped open Stinko's knife and plunged it into Mariani's right hand, pinning it to the wooden desk. Mariani screamed in pain. Martisse screamed in horror. Left hand shaking, Mariani pulled the bloody knife out of the desk and wrapped his perforated hand in a handkerchief.

"And let that be a lesson to you," said Albert.

They put the two kilos in my knapsack (why *me*?). Then we grabbed all our stuff and backed out of there, with Albert and Aziz keeping their guns on the Marianis until we were out of the office. Once in the hallway, Albert slammed the office door shut and we hightailed it out to the waiting taxi. In the cab, Martisse checked her purse. Everything was there, including her small stash of heroin and the zippered leather case containing her "works" (all the paraphernalia she needed to shoot up: Hypodermic, tourniquet, eyedropper, spoon, alcohol, cotton balls). She started to unpack it in the taxi, but Albert hissed, "Non!" and made her put it away.

Once on the train, Martisse headed straight for the bathroom, clutching her purse. I jumped up and headed her off, blocking her access to the loo. "Don't do it, Martisse! You've been through the worst of it, now's your chance to quit." But she shoved me out of the way with a savage determination and locked herself in the ladies' room. I pounded on the door. "Please, Martisse, save yourself!" No answer. I went back to the compartment where Albert and Aziz sat, impassive. "You should have helped me stop her," I said.

"Why?" asked Albert with a snort. "She is our best customer."

After that, I wanted nothing more to do with them. I took the two kilos of heroin out of my knapsack and threw them in Albert's lap.

"You can take your shit and go straight to hell!" I said.

I took my knapsack and stormed out of the compartment. I walked toward the back of the train and found a seat in a compartment with a family of German tourists; a mother, father, boy about eight, and little girl, maybe five. "May I sit here?" I asked.

"Yes," said the father. He spoke English. "You travel alone?"

"Yes."

I saw Albert walk by in the corridor and give me the eye.

"Did you like Marseille?"

"Oh, yes. It was *swell*!"

Then they all chattered merrily in German. I heard the two kids quote me using the word "svell" and laugh uproariously. I smiled good-naturedly and took out my book.

When we reached the Gare de Lyon, I bade my companions *auf wiedersehen* and tried to blend into the crowd exiting the train, but it was no use. Albert, Aziz, and Martisse were waiting for me at the entrance to the big waiting room. Albert had his hand in his pocket and I knew there was a gun in it. He raised it in my direction.

"Now, you are going to behave, yes?"

He spun me around roughly and shoved the two kilos, which were now in a brown paper bag, into my knapsack. I had no choice but to walk with them out to the taxi. I didn't retrieve my suitcase from the locker. It was much safer where it was.

Back at Martisse's building, I was ushered into Mme LaBrot's office behind the front desk. The thugs took the heroin from my knapsack and plopped it down on Mme LaBrot's desk. She looked at me and smiled creepily.

"You did well, mon petit. You 'ave des couilles!"

She was telling me I had balls.

"'ow would you like a job?"

"No thanks," I said. "Am I free to go now?"

"Oui."

I looked at Martisse balefully.

"Adieu, Martisse."

I wanted to say more, but I couldn't find the words. I wouldn't say them in front of this crowd anyway. She looked at the floor for a long moment, then up at me with fire and tears in her eyes.

"Fine, go!"

V I walked slowly toward the Café Dupont, pondering my options. I had that terrible sinking feeling again, like when I let Robin go. I fished the two wrinkled slips of paper out of my pocket. One had the address and phone number of Irving Moskowitz, aka author Nick DuMornay, the other, Charlotte, the blonde actress. These two were now my only possible lifelines in Paris. I decided to call Irving. No possibility of another messy relationship there. And besides, he might give me some pointers on writing. I had now finished *Cool City*, and I was anxious for the opportunity to discuss it with him.

It was almost four in the afternoon when I arrived at Café Dupont. I made straight for the payphone and dialed Irving's number. It just rang and rang. Perhaps he was hanging out at the Sélect. I decided to walk over there.

He was. Irving was holding court at the long table in the Sélect. Gathered around him was a motley assortment of young writers and artists. They were arguing about New Wave cinema and who was a better director: Jean-Luc Godard or Françios Truffaut. But somehow Irving was able to steer the conversation to the racial injustice in the United States, and from there to his protagonist, Danny, and to his book, *Cool City*. I waved to Irving and took a seat at the table. I mentioned that I had just finished the book and thought it was exceptional. Irving gave me a big smile and indicated for me to take the empty chair next to him, so I did. He was manic and expansive. He ordered another carafe of *vin rouge* and a glass for me.

By seven, Irving's crowd of acolytes had thinned to me and two others, a guy and girl, both in their twenties. They were both Americans. Peter was from New York and shared many of my old haunts. Eve was from San Francisco. Peter and Irving had both been there, and there was a brief discussion about the beauties of that city.

Finally, it was down to me and Irving. He was pretty drunk at this point, and I was definitely feeling the effect of the wine. He suggested we go to a restaurant he liked called Café Procope in Saint-Germain.

It was old and elegant and really, really good. I had never had pâte foie gras, and I loved it. Until I found out how it was made. The place was not cheap. I offered to chip in, but Irving insisted on picking up the tab.

He chain-smoked Gauloises. I accepted one or two from him since I was out of my American smokes. They had a harsh, acrid taste, but they were incredibly popular over here, along with Gitanes.

We talked about *Cool City*, about his character, Danny. I asked him how he came up with the idea for the book. "All good fiction starts with at least a grain of truth," he said. It turns out he had worked as a parole officer in the New York Police Department's Juvenile Division, one of many jobs on his long, strange résumé. "Danny is based on a real kid I had as one of my 'clients'," he said. "I got him a job on a farm in New Jersey, which ultimately broke the cycle of violence in his life."

"Oh, so that's where the farm in the book came from?"

"Yeah. It didn't work out so well in the book. I needed to add more conflict there, but it did in real life."

He asked me how things had gone with my "girlfriend."

"Martisse?" I sighed. "It didn't work out with her. I was crazy about her. Still am, but she's bad news. Listen," I said, "that offer to crash at your place. Does it still stand?"

"Certainly. I have a large apartment with a spare room and no roommates but my cat, Raskolnikov."

I smiled at the name—one of my favorite characters in all of literature.

"That's great," I said. "I really appreciate it."

Sitting across from us, a man was reading *Le Parisien*. On page three was my picture. The same one the cops had at the train station. The headline was hard to read, but I was able to make out POLICE SEEK…

It was a short walk from the restaurant to chez Irving, which was on rue de l'Éperon. This was the high-rent district of the Left Bank, close to the Seine. The building was sort of a squared-off triangle with the front door at the apex, where rue de l'Éperon and rue Suger, two quaint, narrow streets, converged. The place had high ceilings, and in the spacious living room there dangled an ancient crystal chandelier. But that was about all. It smelled of cat pee. There was barely a stick of furniture; just vast wooden floors covered in dust. He had a desk, a chair, and a typewriter by the tall windows, a ratty couch against the far wall, and instead of a coffee table, there was an upsidedown orange crate. He showed me the room where I was to sleep. It was small and dirty. There was nothing but an unmade cot. There was the master bedroom where Raskolnikov, a large black-and-white tomcat, lounged on the rumpled bed, and the bathroom from which the cat smell emanated. He ushered me back to the living room, and I settled onto the sofa while he went into the equally-squalid kitchen, with its sink full of dirty dishes, and opened yet another bottle of red wine. My glass looked a bit murky, but as I was already three sheets to the wind, I drank. I would have thought Irving had made a bundle off *Cool City*, but good manners prevented me from quizzing him on this.

"Sorry, the place is a bit untidy. I need to get a housekeeper—and some furniture." He laughed.

Silently, I resolved that, when I get my own place, it will be neat, clean, and smell nice. Eventually, I got up the nerve to show him my journal. I told him how it had started as just a diary of my travels but had soon morphed into a work of fiction and fantasy. "I started writing in the third person, about a kid my age named Frankie and his adventures in Europe. It certainly has more than a grain of truth."

"Would you like me to read it?" he asked.

"Would you? I don't know if you can read my writing, but…"

He took the book from me. "Yeah. Your writing's not as sloppy as mine." And he commenced reading.

While he read, I got up and looked out the window at the deserted street below. I started weaving, so I pulled up the rickety desk chair and sat. Suddenly, a great sadness washed over me that even the wine could not dispel. I thought of Robin, back in New York by now, about to start at Cooper Union. I knew that building well. It was on Astor Place, where St. Marks Place turns into 8th Street. I had walked that way dozens of times on my way to the Village. Then I started thinking about Martisse. And worrying. She was in a terrible, dark place, and I wanted badly to save her.

But you can't save someone unless they want to be saved. Was it possible to love two women at once? After a while, my musings were penetrated by the sound of Irving's voice.

"What a story!" he was saying. "Did all this stuff in Marseille really happen?"

"Yes, it really did."

"Amazing! The writing could use some polish, but I think you've got the beginnings of something really good here, Eddie."

"Wow. Thanks, Irving! You don't know what that means to me."

"Yes, I do. Now, here's what I suggest: Write the whole book out longhand like you're doing. Don't worry too much about the writing style or the wording; just get the story down. Then, get a typewriter and type it up. While you're typing, you can make revisions and polish it. But wait a bit after you've finished the longhand version. Let it settle—'percolate' I call it—before you start typing. I find time gives you the distance you need to see your flaws—and virtues—more clearly. Oh, and one more thing: You should know how the book ends. You may not know what will happen next, but you should definitely know how and where you're going to end up. You might even consider writing a draft of the final scene before you finish."

We talked a while longer—I think I mentioned wanting to go to the station and get my stuff—and then I passed out on the couch. Irving didn't wake me to go to the bed, and it's just as well. The couch seemed a little cleaner than the bed, although it did smell of stale tobacco smoke and booze.

Sometime later—I don't know what time—I was awakened by gentle caresses on my private parts. At first, I thought I was dreaming of Martisse. Gradually, I realized it was not a dream. I sat bolt upright. And there was Irving, kneeling beside the couch, feeling me up!

"What the hell, Irving!"

"What? I wasn't doing anything. Just watching you sleep." He was very drunk and slurring his words.

"The hell you say. You were touching me!"

"You only dreamed it."

"Bullshit! I'm getting out of here!" I jumped to my feet, grabbed my knapsack, and ran for the door.

"Hey, wait!" Irving cried after me. But I was out in the hallway and down the stairs in a flash.

I couldn't believe Irving was *queer*. Another illusion shattered, another bridge burned. Oh, I didn't care if somebody was gay. "À chacun son goût," as we say in France (to each his own). The thought of two guys having sex nauseated me, but I would never pass judgment on others—as long as they were consenting adults. But I was *not* consenting. And I guess I wasn't an adult, though I hate to admit it. *Now* what?

It was three o'clock in the morning, and I had no place to go. I thought of trying to call Charlotte—the last Paris phone number I had left—but showing up on her doorstep at three a.m. would make me look desperate and pathetic (which I was). I started back toward Montparnasse. The streets were nearly deserted. A hooker smoked in a doorway. The "Boule Saint-Miche" was only a couple of blocks away, so I followed it down past the Café Dupont, which had recently closed. A group of artists was still out front, arguing about Giacometti. When I got to the Luxembourg Gardens, something made me turn off onto rue Soufflot, then onto a smaller street, rue le Goff, then onto the even-smaller rue Malebranche. And there I saw it. A sign in a first-floor window of a run-down building: CHAMBRE À LOUER (room for rent). Of course, it was too late to inquire, so I wrote down the address—17 rue Malebranche—and decided to wait in the park until a decent hour.

I sat on a bench in the Luxembourg Gardens. Then, I lay down and fell asleep with my knapsack under my head.

I awoke with a start. A gendarme was tapping on my foot with his nightstick. I quickly put on my prop glasses and sat up. But he just told me I couldn't sleep there and moved on.

At nine, I walked back to 17 rue Malebranche and rang the bell. A well-groomed woman of about fifty with graying hair and sharp, kind eyes opened the door.

"Good morning, Madame. Your room for rent," I said in French, "may I see it?"

The lobby had the usual concierge desk and a telephone mounted on one wall. It was old but very clean and well-kept. There was no elevator. She led me up two flights of creaky stairs to the third floor and unlocked a door with a brass number nine on it. The room was a decent size and had a large window that looked out onto the street and let in plenty of light. Outside the window was a small balcony, just wide enough for a few plants, which appeared to be flourishing. There was a table, a bed, a dresser, a washbasin, and its own private WC (a big plus). I tested the bed. It had clean sheets and was neatly made up with a couple of soft blankets.

"How much?" I asked.

"Twenty-eight francs a week, monsieur. In advance," she said. That was roughly seven dollars. "I change the bedding once a week and will do your laundry for an additional three francs."

"I'll take it." I pulled the money out of my jeans and handed it to her. I gave her the extra three francs for laundry. Then I extended my hand. "Je m'appelle Jesse. Jesse Bright."

"Madame Benoit." She shook my hand. "Êtes vous français?"

"Non, américain." *Shit! I should have said English.* I just had to hope she didn't ask to see my passport.

Then she squinted at me. "Juif?" She was asking me if I was Jewish.

"Uh…oui…" I answered tentatively. *I don't look especially Jewish. How could she know?*

She smiled and broke into very good English. "Come for dinner tomorrow night at seven. I'm making my famous chicken soup."

I thanked her and said I would come (I could never refuse free food). She gave me keys to the front door and to my room, told me the bathroom (where there was a bathtub with a shower) was two doors down the hall, and departed. *These Jews*, I thought, *they're everywhere!*

I sat on my new bed and looked out the window. Across the narrow street was a synagogue.

VI The next day was Tuesday. I left my room and set out for the Gare de Lyon to get my suitcase and sleeping bag. On the stairs, I met one of my neighbors. He was coming up as I was going down; an old man, maybe sixty, thin, with white hair and beard. We exchanged "bon jours" and that was it.

Once on the street, I realized that, if I followed rue Malebranche just one block east, I would be on Martisse's street. Was this an accident, or something in my subconscious?

I flagged down a taxi on "Boule'Miche" and headed for the station, wearing my prop glasses and carrying my Brit passport. I asked the cabby to wait while I went in and retrieved my stuff. I bought another newspaper—*Le Parisien*, the one that had my picture. Then, back to my room.

I reveled in my newfound peace and privacy, although I could hear someone moving around in the room upstairs. I spent the rest of the day sitting at the little table writing. I forgot about the newspaper. At seven, I was very hungry and went downstairs to Mme Benoit's spacious apartment for dinner.

I learned that she was a widow, but she introduced me to her son, Alain: About twenty, short, dark, brooding eyes, unsmiling. He lived with her.

"Enchanté," I said, shaking his hand.

He gave me a limp handshake and curt nod. At dinner, we spoke English.

"Where in America are you from?" asked Mme Benoit.

"New York City." Alain had put me off, so I was more circumspect than usual.

"Ah, you were there, Alain," Mme Benoit eagerly chimed in. "Souvien-toi?" (Remember?)

"Of course," said Alain, still sullen.

"He won the famous Young Concert Artists Award at Carnegie Hall two years ago," Mme Benoit beamed, "Alain is a concert violinist."

"Oh, I've heard of that award. That's amazing, Alain," I said, trying to get a rise out of him.

He just grunted.

"Will I hear you play?"

"I don't play anymore." He gave me an angry, defiant look, daring me to ask why. I didn't press the matter any further. Mme Benoit looked embarrassed.

"Your chicken soup deserves its fame," I told her.

"I'll get the pot roast," she said.

Her pot roast and potatoes were also spectacular, and I told her so.

"Would you like to come to temple with us Friday? It's right across the street."

"Yes, I saw it. Thank you, but no. I'm not religious."

"You don't have to be religious," she started to continue, but Alain cut her off.

"Leave him alone, Mother. If he's not one of us, he's not."

I bristled. "I am one of you—by heredity. I can't help that. But religiously, I'm not. That's my choice."

"You should have been here during the war," he said. "You'd feel differently then."

"But you were just a baby during the war," I said. "How would you know?"

"Tell him, Mother."

Mme Benoit, almost apologetically, said, "In 1943, the year Alain was born, the *Milice*, French Nazis, took us from our home—we had a nice place then. They took everything we had. I managed to bribe a truck driver to take Alain and me to Switzerland. My husband refused to go. They shot him."

"That's terrible," I said. "I can't imagine what that must have been like…"

"That's right, you can't," said Alain. "And, to this day, the French are as antisemitic as any race on Earth."

"Well," I said, "if I experienced what you did, I might feel as you do. But my experience growing up in New York was very different—although the Irish Catholic kids did pick on us Jews."

"Oh, I'm sure that was horrible," said Alain sarcastically.

"No," said I, "it was a good lesson for me. I learned something about bullies. If you stand up to them—even if they beat the shit out of you—I beg your pardon, Mme Benoit—after a while they leave you alone. Bullies are cowards. If you give them a fight, even if you lose, it becomes too inconvenient for them, and they pick on easier targets. Like all my Jewish friends, who cowered in fear before the fight even started. And that's why I quit the Jews."

"Well," said Alain, "take a look at the Israelis. Are they cowering in fear?"

"No. And I'm rooting for them."

After that, the conversation drifted into the mundane and finally tapered off altogether. I thanked the Benoits for their hospitality and went upstairs to my room.

I opened *Le Parisien*, and there, on the second page, was a picture of the latest victim of "Le Tueur de Prostituées." It was Martisse. My heart froze. And then it broke. My chest felt heavy, constricted. I tried to swallow, gasped for air. All our times together raced through my mind. I felt a single tear run down my left cheek. I really had loved her. I loved her still. Hooker, junkie, I didn't care. She was smart and brave and had love in her heart. I wondered if she ever loved me. I liked to think she did. I didn't believe in God or an afterlife, but I found myself praying she was in a better place than she was with Mme LaBrot and her minions. Nobody this close to me had ever died. Through my tears, I envisioned a scenario where I went and confronted LaBrot, Albert, and Aziz and accused them of being the cause of Martisse's death. But, of course, that would serve no purpose now—except maybe to get me killed.

I poured over the details of the crime again and again. The murder had taken place right in her room, right in the bed in which she and I had slept. I envisioned the scene soaked in blood. The killer had used a large kitchen knife.

I sat at my table-desk and wrote a poem to Martisse:

Where are you, my Dirty Angel?
Did they give you wings?
Maybe rusty, dusty wings
I hope you hover someplace near
Where you can watch my foolish antics
And laugh

Then I translated it into French, so Martisse could understand it better. Writing the poem helped lighten the weight of my grief, and I felt better.

Then I began to devise a revenge plan. I contrived to track down the killer and kill him the same bloody way he had killed Martisse.

It harkened back to the summer I was eight. My family was at one of those bungalow colonies north of New York City. I was lucky; since my parents were both teachers, they got the whole summer off. They got me a kitten. I loved it dearly. It was tiny and playful and the light of my life. Then, one morning, my father broke the news that my cat had been killed by a raccoon. See, my mother was allergic to cats, so they made it sleep outside on the ground. It was killed as it slept. I never got to see the mess that was left; my father cleaned it all up before I could see it. I knew the raccoons frequented the communal garbage dump so after that I patrolled the garbage dump, armed with a baseball bat. I was fully prepared to bash the raccoon's head in if I saw it. The real objects of my hatred were my parents—but that was an inconvenient truth I was not prepared to face.

Of course, the whole revenge notion was absurd.

The next day, I decided to go out and look for a used typewriter. In a neighborhood with a lot of antique and second-hand shops, I found an old Royal. I tested it and all the keys worked, so I bought it, with carrying case, for twelve francs. I was able to find a ream of cheap paper and an extra ink ribbon at a stationers. On the way back, I passed a lamppost with a poster stuck on it for *Hedda Gabler* at the American Theater, starring that new acting sensation, Charlotte Livingston. I could've hit her up for a free pass, but I decided to buy a ticket and show up unannounced. Much classier. It was Wednesday, and the next performance was Friday night. I went over to the theater box office and purchased a ticket for eight francs. Then, I took my new used typewriter home. As I entered my building, I encountered Alain, looking agitated, rushing out. He brushed past me without so much as a bonjour.

I set the typewriter up on my writing table. I was tempted to start typing my Frankie Walz story right away, but remembering Irving's advice, I decided to keep writing it in longhand until I had finished the first draft.

I now had nothing to read, having finished Irving's book. It was still early afternoon, so I decided to get some lunch at the Café Dupont and then walk to Quai Voltaire to the *bouquinistes*—the outdoor book market—in Saint-Germain.

I couldn't find much in English, and I wasn't confident enough in written French to try to read a whole book in it. I finally found a dog-eared copy of Hemingway's *The Sun Also Rises* in English, and I bought it for one franc.

Summer was over. It was now September, and it began to rain. I didn't have a proper raincoat or umbrella, so I stopped on the way home and bought both items at a used clothing shop. The raincoat was a bit large, but it did the job. Back in my room, I counted the cash I had left. Just under 3,000 francs. I had already burned through 200. I realized I'd have to find some kind of income or invest a big chunk of what I had left in a return ticket to America—insurance against being broke and stranded in France. I gave myself a week to get some kind of off-the-books job. If I failed, I would buy the ticket.

With Martisse gone and Irving a pervert, I suddenly felt very much alone in Paris. I had no idea what Charlotte's attitude toward me would be. She seemed so mercurial, but I hoped she would at least remember me.

Mme Benoit knocked on my door and invited me for Shabbas dinner Friday night, but I politely declined. That was the night of the play. Besides, that Alain gave me the creeps. I opened my journal and tried to continue my story, but I realized I didn't know where to go with it. I started reading the Hemingway book. I had only read *The Old Man and the Sea*, which I liked. I liked his short, pithy sentences and unpretentious, plain-English style. But as *The Sun Also Rises* unfolded, it seemed as though Hemingway, too, really didn't know where to take the story. It was very light on plot and heavy on character development. Beyond a bunch of American and British ex-pats wandering aimlessly around Paris, and then Spain, there wasn't much to it. It had caused a literary sensation in its time, but I didn't see why. Maybe it was because his voice was so different from the ornate prose prevalent in the twenties.

On Friday, I wondered if I should get some flowers and present them to Charlotte after her performance. But then I thought that would be too unlike me—too flowery. So I took a shower, dressed in my one sports coat, white shirt, and tie, and set off for the theater. As bad luck would have it, I ran into Mme Benoit and Alain in the lobby as they were leaving for Friday night services. "Oh, hello, Jesse," said Mme Benoit, "and where are you off to?" I explained that a friend of mine was in a play. I didn't elaborate further. As usual, Alain just silently glowered at me. "Well, *Shabbat shalom*," she said.

"Bon soir," said I and walked off into the night.

Too bad, I thought, *I love my room, but these people are getting intrusive.* I decided to start looking around for something else.

The house was not packed, but I'd say it was a good turnout. It seems the show had opened the previous Friday and had received a number of favorable reviews, mostly in English-language publications. Charlotte did not disappoint. I was very impressed with her performance. A born thespian, that's what she was.

When I went backstage, she was besieged with admirers, so I took my place in the queue. I wasn't sure she would remember me, but she did. She gave me a hug and thanked me for coming. "I wanted to get you a ticket for opening night," she said. "That was a week ago. Where have you been?"

"You wouldn't believe it if I told you," I said. "You were really great." I didn't have to pad my praise; it was true.

A few others from her crowd were there as well: Her roommate Meg, Jean-Marc the writer, and Brian the Brit painter. They invited me to come along to their hangout, le Sélect, and I happily joined them.

I now looked at Charlotte with new eyes, new respect. Her artistry had dazzled me, and now *she* began to dazzle me. I began to entertain romantic notions, but I saw the way Brian was looking at her, and I suspected there was something between her and the tall, blond artist. I'd be sorry competition for him. At their usual table, a few more of the group I had gone to the party with were already assembled.

The talk was all about the murders. They all knew about Martisse and told me how sorry they were to hear about my friend. It brought the whole thing crashing back to the forefront of my mind, and I almost broke down again.

"I need to make some money," I said, changing the subject. "Does anybody know of an under-the-table job?"

"Under the table?" asked Jean-Marc.

"Yeah. Cash. No checks, no taxes. Er, see, I don't want certain people to be able to find me."

"Oh. You're 'on the lam,' huh?" said Meg, joking.

"Actually, yes," I said. "Please don't ask me any more questions. I just need a little help."

"Talk to Jacques," said Brian. "Maybe you can work here."

"That's a great idea," I said and headed for the kitchen.

Jacques remembered me. "Ah, le petit américain!" He called me "the little American." Not too insulting, given that Jacques was enormous, both vertically and horizontally. I asked him for a job, and he told me he needed a new dishwasher. "The Algerian guy, he's disappeared. Damn Algerians. Very unreliable," he said. "Are you willing to wash dishes?"

"Oui."

"Okay. I pay you three francs an hour. You start Monday."

"How many hours?" I asked.

"Three nights a week, from five p.m. to three a.m."

Ten hours a night of washing dishes. It sounded dismal, but thirty hours a week would get me ninety francs. I could live on that.

"D'accord," I said and went back and shook Brian the Brit's hand. "Madames et monsieurs, you are now looking at the new head dishwasher at le Café Sélect!"

Everyone applauded. "Hooray, Eddie!" they cried.

"Oh, one more thing: Call me Jesse."

I bought two carafes of wine for everyone and we all toasted my good fortune.

Charlotte pulled me aside. "Would you like to see the play again?"

"Sure." I was gazing into her lovely blue eyes, and she was gazing back.

"Come tomorrow night. I'll leave a ticket for you at the box office."

"Under the name Jesse Bright."

"Right...Jesse." She gave me a smile that had my heart racing. Perhaps I did have a chance with her.

"Hey, I got a place of my own. Want to see it?"

"Now?"

"Yeah."

"I can't tonight. Maybe tomorrow."

I wondered if she really meant it. After all the wine and my great uptick in fortunes, I walked home feeling better than I had in quite a while.

As I approached my building, I saw a small, shadowy figure dart out the front door and down the steps. In spite of the long, dark overcoat and broad-brimmed fedora, I immediately recognized it as Alain. I ducked into a doorway. A terrible foreboding now filled my heart. Where the hell was he going at two o'clock in the morning? I thought about following him but decided against it. I couldn't bring myself to believe that little gremlin was the hooker killer. And there was something else; something I hesitate, even now, to admit: I didn't want to get involved with anything that would put me in the sights of the law. See, even if Alain was the one, by identifying him, I would also be identified and sent back into the arms of my parents and the good old U.S. of A.

But that night, as I lay awake unable to sleep, I wondered if he might really be the killer. If he was, I owed it to Martisse to get him. I got out of bed, put on some clothes, and went out into the hallway. As silently as possible, I descended the stairs and found a door under the staircase that led to the basement. There was no sound but a couple of tomcats outside yowling at each other. I huddled inside the basement door, leaving it open just enough to hear and see anyone entering the building. I stayed there for maybe ninety minutes. Then the front door opened and in walked Alain. I could just make out that he appeared to be concealing something under his coat. Then the soft thud of something hitting the carpeted floor. Alain quickly bent to pick it up, and in that instant, I could see the flash of a blade. The blade of a large kitchen knife.

Alain quickly disappeared into his mother's apartment. When I was sure he was gone, I came out and examined the place where the knife had dropped. There was a damp red spot there. Blood.

Late the next morning I awoke from a fitful sleep. On my way to brunch at the Café Dupont, I checked the spot on the carpet. It was just damp, but no trace of blood. At the café, I picked up a discarded copy of *Le Parisien*. It carried the banner headline: LE TUEUR DE PROSTITUÉES FRAPPE À NOUVEAU! (Hooker Killer Strikes Again!). It had happened in a seedy part of Montparnasse, not a quarter-mile from where I sat. The M.O. was the same. The poor girl was butchered in her own bed with a large kitchen knife, just like the one Mme Benoit used to cook her delicious pot roast. The police had no clues.

It was Alain, for sure. My mind raced. How could I nail him without getting nailed myself? It was all I could think about.

That night, I went to see the play again, and Charlotte.

She played to a packed house and rousing ovation. After the champagne and adoration in the dressing room, we headed once again to le Sélect, this time with a somewhat larger entourage. All the members of the group I had met ten days ago were present, as well as some new faces.

Charlotte was plainly soaking it up, and she deserved it. This was her shining moment, perhaps the only one she'd ever get, although I was pretty sure she would go on to even greater heights. We drank toast after toast to "la nouvelle Sarah Bernhardt."

The events of last night had put a damper on what would have been my delicious anticipation at the prospect of her coming home with me. Now, I wasn't sure I wanted her to be in my building, let alone my room. I didn't want her anywhere near Alain.

As it turned out, I needn't have been concerned about this. Tonight, Charlotte only had eyes for Brian the Brit. I might as well have been part of the wallpaper. She now gazed into his eyes the way she had gazed into mine only last night. The only acknowledgment I received from her was a vague hello, and she seemed to look right through me as she said it. Now, my anguish was twofold. I didn't know what to feel worse about: Not knowing how to stop Alain or being ignored by Charlotte. I decided to call it a night and made my way home. My departure was noted by no one.

VII

I decided to focus on my writing and my job. Monday was my first night washing dishes for le Sélect. I discovered that being compulsively thorough was not an asset in this job. It made me too slow, and the dishes piled up faster than I could clean them. At three-thirty a.m., soaked in sweat, I dragged myself home, took a shower, and went to bed.

My plan was to stay in and write during my waking hours. I turned into the cliché of a depressed, reclusive writer. I was writing about Martisse, her murder, Alain, Paris, Charlotte, rejection, loneliness. On the four nights of the week I was not slaving away at the Sélect, I kept an eye out for Alain.

When I went to le Sélect, I often saw Irving and his followers or Charlotte and her followers, or both at once. We acknowledged each other with a barely perceptible nod. I just walked straight into the kitchen and never attempted to speak with either of them. Sometimes Brian or Jean-Marc would say hello, and I would say hello back. I gradually settled into a dreary half-life of washing dishes, sleeping, eating, and writing my story half-assedly. The initial flush of inspiration had vanished, but still I trudged on; not sure why. I read when I could get a decent book on the cheap, and the work of writers like Hemmingway, Thomas Wolfe, Chekov, and Fitzgerald only depressed me more. I could never be that good.

Still, I had a story to tell, and I would tell it the best way I knew how. I was still in the hand-writing stage. Following Irving's advice, I would not start typing until I had the whole book in longhand on paper. I was using pencils down to the nub, and sometimes I would go right through the paper with my eraser.

I picked up a copy of *Le Parisien* every day to see if Alain had killed anyone else. So far, no new murders.

I wrote a letter to my parents. I figured I owed them that much at least. I told them that I was working and supporting myself and trying to write. "Don't blame yourselves," I wrote. "This decision had nothing to do with the way you brought me up. All my life, something in my nature has driven me to seek complete freedom, for better or for worse. I hope you can get your money back from Chandler. I have made and lost several friends in the short time I've been here, and I now lead a very solitary life. If and when I feel I've accomplished my writing goals, I will return to New York. I will soon turn 18 and will then be considered an adult. At that time, I will give you my address. Paris is surely the most beautiful city in the world. Maybe you can come and visit me here someday.

Love,

Eddie."

Even on my nights off, my schedule had become nocturnal. I was now accustomed to sleeping most of the day and staying up most of the night. I had little interaction with Mme Benoit. I would leave the rent money in an envelope in her box every week, and she would—per my instructions—come in and change the bedding and take my laundry every week on Monday night when I was at work. Every day about three p.m., I would walk over to the Café Dupont and eat my main meal, usually eggs. On my off-nights, I sat at my writing table and glanced out the window from time to time. One night, I saw Alain go out late. I decided to follow him.

By the time I got downstairs, he had disappeared around the corner onto rue le Goff. I ran to catch up and reached rue le Goff just in time to see him turn again onto rue Soufflot and walk fast toward the Luxembourg Gardens. I followed at a discreet distance. At this hour, there was not much traffic on the Boul'Miche, but as luck would have it, he hailed a taxi, got in, and drove north. I frantically searched the boulevard for another cab, but by the time I spotted one, it was too late. He was gone—headed, no doubt, toward the red-light district near Place Pigalle in the sleazy heart of the city.

Sure enough, the next day *Le Parisien* carried another "Prostituée Tueur" story. This time, he had struck in the Pigalle district. *I wish I had a gun. If killing him is the only way to stop this maniac, I'll do it!*

Then it came to me. I wouldn't have to do it myself; all I needed to do was walk down the block and see Mme LaBrot. Instead of accusing her, I would enlist her. Albert and Aziz would do the job. And it wouldn't necessarily have to be pure revenge for them. As long as Alain was roaming the streets, their other girls were also in peril. I went to see Mme LaBrot.

"You are sure of this?" she queried after hearing my story.

"Absolutely. I saw the bloody knife fall from his hand. Every time he goes out late, another girl gets killed."

A look of frightening resolve came over her face. "Très bien. It shall be done…" Then she teared up. "…pour ma chère Martisse!"

So, it would be a revenge killing after all. For me, too.

One night, about two a.m., I saw Alain go out. He didn't come back. Two days later, the police showed up to talk to Mme Benoit. They interviewed all the tenants in the building, including me, asking if they had any idea of his whereabouts. I told them I hadn't seen him in quite a while. I knew the deed was done. Alain would never be found, and the hooker killings would stop.

When I passed Mme Benoit in the hallways, she looked more and more distraught every time I saw her. I felt a mixture of guilt and exhilaration. I didn't like causing this nice lady pain, but if she knew the truth, I was sure she'd understand why it had to be done. Nah. We're talking about a Jewish mother and her son here. She'd never understand.

One day, she buttonholed me going up the stairs and asked to speak with me. Once inside her apartment, she broke down.

"Where is he?" she sobbed. "Why can't they find him?"

"I-I'm sorry, Mme Benoit, I have no idea."

"Maybe he went to Israel. He was always talking about joining some elite Israeli commando group and fighting the Arabs. But why would he disappear without a word?"

I shrugged. "I don't know."

I wondered how to recount these events in my book. I would have to make up something completely false. The truth was one hell of a good story, but of course, I couldn't tell it.

Instead, I made up a wonderful story that entailed a taxi chase through the red-light district and an anonymous phone call to the cops. They caught him red-handed—literally. I made myself look like a big hero, without actually hurting anybody. In my book, Alain got his just desserts at the hands of the law. The hands of Frankie Walz, at least, were clean.

At the Café Dupont, my habitual brunch spot, I struck up a conversation with two young American guys, Bert Connor and Jerry Woolsey, fellow writers. Bert, tall and thin with sandy blond hair and an aristocratic nose, was a journalist. He worked part-time for the *International Herald-Tribune*, the preeminent English language newspaper in France, writing book and theatrical reviews. I asked him if he had seen the American Theater production of *Hedda Gabler*. He had and had given Charlotte rave reviews. Unable to resist bragging, I told them I knew her. Bert and Jerry were both very keen to meet her. I said she could be found most nights at le Sélect and that I would introduce them. I regretted this almost immediately. Why would I want to go sniffing around Charlotte again after she had given me the cold shoulder? Some kind of subconscious kamikaze deathwish, I supposed.

Jerry, a short guy with curly hair, an outsized nose, and glasses, was an aspiring novelist like me. We talked about our own work, our favorite writers, and our hopes for the future. He told me about a great American novelist by the name of Kurt Vonnegut. Under the veneer of science fiction, Vonnegut was really writing social commentary, decrying the ignorance, greed and hypocrisy so prevalent in America, and especially the American Midwest, where Vonnegut hailed from. Jerry had just finished his newest book, *Cat's Cradle*. It was a dark comedy about how the bumbling of one absent-minded scientist sets off a chain reaction that brings about the end of the world. He had the book with him and showed it to me. After five solid minutes of begging, Jerry agreed to lend it to me. I assured him I would return it unscathed and could be found right here every day around three. I gave them both my home address and the phone number of the hall telephone. Bert gave me his business card, and Jerry made one for me, replete with a wonderful caricature of himself, all nose and spectacles. It was good to make some new friends after my weeks of isolation and estrangement. We all agreed to meet the following night at the Sélect. It would be my first appearance there on my night off. I hoped Charlotte wouldn't humiliate me in front of my new pals.

The next night—Tuesday—the usual crowd was gathered around the big table at the Sélect. Charlotte's play was still running. The theater only operated Fridays through Sundays, so tonight was her night off, as well as mine. I hung by the entrance and observed from afar. Charlotte was holding court as usual. She was recounting, with great hilarity, how she had blown her second line on the opening night of the play.

"...so, Miss Tesman asks me if 'the new bride has slept well in her new home,' and I'm supposed to reply, 'Oh yes, thanks—passably.' And I say, 'Oh yes, thanks—possibly'!"

Everyone laughed, with Charlotte laughing the loudest.

"I must have been turning beet red," she said, "but everyone went on without a hiccup, and no one in the audience seemed to even notice. Actually, now that I think of it, I'm not so sure that line wasn't better!"

More loud laughter. At that moment, Bert and Jerry showed up. The three of us approached the big table and stood opposite Charlotte. I cleared my throat.

"Uh, Charlotte, I'd like you to meet Bert Connor and Jerry Woolsey. They're big fans of yours."

"Hello," said Charlotte, looking at me strangely. "Won't you all join us?"

"Bert wrote that glowing review of your performance in the *Herald-Tribune*," I said. She lapped it up.

"Oh, in that case, Bert, why don't you come sit over here by me? I want you to tell me all about yourself." She leaned over and whispered to Meg, who sat on her left, and Meg scooted her chair over to make room for Bert.

I swear, what a self-involved, egomaniacal phony! As Bert eagerly moved his chair next to Charlotte, I smiled and nodded in her direction, never betraying a trace of bitterness.

Jerry, who was quite the wit, chimed in, "I didn't write any reviews of you, Charlotte. Should I go sit in the corner?"

"Yes!" said Charlotte gleefully, and she pointed to the corner. "Sit there and face the wall!"

And Jerry moved his chair to the corner and faced the wall, amidst uproarious laughter. This set the tone for an evening of much hilarity and vin rouge. By two a.m., my head was spinning. I wanted to talk to Charlotte, to get a few things off my chest, so when "our song," Dexter Gordon's "Willow Weep for Me," came on the jukebox (the Sélect had a very hip jukebox), I weaved my way around the table and approached Charlotte, hands outstretched.

"C'mon, Charlotte, they're playing our song," I said.

She rolled her eyes but obliged.

As we danced (she didn't hold me close like she had at the party), I couldn't resist making up a poem for her:

"Charlotte, Oh, Charlotte, now that you're a starlet

Are you too important to dance with me?

Charlotte, Oh, Charlotte, someone killed my harlot

Take pity on this drunken fool, I swear I don't have fleas."

She looked at me and I thought she was going to slap my face, but instead she cracked up, laughing hysterically.

"You just made that up? That's really good, Eddie—um, er, Jesse. Really funny. You're quite a talent, mon petit chou-chou."

"I'm glad I din't piss ya off," I slurred. "You're quite a talon yourself, Char. Ma petite char-char."

She laughed again. Then I passed out. Right on the dance floor.

Jerry and Bert had to prop me up as we walked home. They wanted me to come to their place, said I could crash on their couch, but I insisted they drag me to my place, which was on their way.

VIII

As I dove into *Cat's Cradle*, I became more and more beguiled by Kurt Vonnegut, by his wit and imagination. I wished my prose had that originality, that electricity. But I was writing fiction based on fact, not the wild flights of fantasy that pervaded Vonnegut's work. How could I absorb and translate that brilliance into my work? I had reached a point in my story where I didn't know where to go next. I had to back away and think about it.

As the days grew colder, I bought a long overcoat and warm sweater. Instead of just plunging into writing each day, I took long walks after my meal at the Dupont. I walked all around Paris. I became a tourist all over again. I saw much of the beautiful art, architecture, and parks I had been ignoring: The Panthéon, a majestic, neo-classical mausoleum for the honored dead of France, was perched high on a hill, a short but arduous walk from my room. Looking up at the triple-domed ceiling made me marvel anew at the incredible ingenuity of people who had lived and created so long ago, and whose work was immortal. A few blocks farther east, on rue Monge, was the Arènes de Lutèce, the circular ruins of a Roman amphitheater where gladiators had faced off in mortal combat in the first century. Not one for guidebooks, I wandered aimlessly. Closer to the river, I stumbled across Les Invalides, a huge complex of buildings and cobble-stoned yards, originally built as a hospital for wounded soldiers. I crossed the beautifully ornamented bridges over the Seine and accidentally discovered well-known and not-so-well-known places and landmarks with long histories about which I knew nothing: the vast Place Vendôme, dominated by the 145-foot Vendôme Column with a larger-than-life Napoleon at its apex, and home to the opulent Hôtel Ritz, a name that had become synonymous with class around the world, la Tour Saint-Jacques, the only remaining part of a sixteenth-century gothic cathedral destroyed during the French Revolution, La Conciergerie, Palais Garnier, beautiful places I couldn't even name. I discovered a secret garden where Louis XVI and Marie Antoinette were supposedly entombed called the Chapelle Expiatoire. In the Père Lachaise cemetery, I discovered the graves of Oscar Wilde, Balzac, Chopin, Colette, and Proust. I lingered in this hallowed ground, wondering, hoping the spirits of these greats might feed me some inspiration. The tourist season was over and the weather was turning cold and damp, and so I had these magical places mostly to myself.

But while I reveled in it, my solitude was also my greatest source of pain. I yearned for love. I imagined I saw Martisse around every corner. Then I started to see Robin as well. I would walk up fast behind a girl with long, blondish hair and peer at her face when I caught up, often causing looks of consternation, if not outright terror. I wondered if love would ever find me again.

I would often rendezvous with Bert and Jerry at the Dupont or Sélect. They were just about my only source of human contact. I made no effort to pursue Charlotte, although I saw her often, and she reverted to an attitude of indifference toward me. In any case, Charlotte was not a person I felt I could trust or depend on. Charlotte couldn't love anybody—except Charlotte.

It turned out that Bert and Jerry had a third roommate in their spacious three-bedroom flat, and that roommate was moving out—returning to the States, they said. They invited me to move in. The rent would be a little bit higher than what I was paying for my austere quarters, but, according to their description, the place was downright palatial. I told them I would seriously consider it.

I was doing just that when I came home one afternoon and found Mme Benoit in my room. She had my suitcase open on the bed and in each hand she held one of my passports. She glared at me. I glared back.

"What is *this*?" she demanded.

"What are you doing going through my *stuff*?" I demanded.

"Which one of these passports is real, and which is a forgery?"

"They're both real," I lied. "I have dual citizenship."

"With two different names?"

I had no ready answer for that.

"Should I call the police?"

"Go ahead. I'll be packed and gone before they get here."

"Not if I hold on to these."

Quick as a flash, I snatched both passports out of her hands. "Now, get out of here. I'm leaving!"

Five minutes later, I was on the street, walking fast with my typewriter and all my luggage toward 60 rue du Cardinal Lemoine—Bert and Jerry's place. As I walked, I thought: *What did Mme Benoit have against me? When Alain dropped the bloody knife who cleaned the carpet? If he had the knife under his coat, wouldn't his clothes be all bloody? Who cleaned up after him? Was Mme Benoit aware of her son's activities? Did she suspect me of knowing—is that why she turned against me?* Further speculation was pointless, as I was out of her life and she was out of mine.

It was a posh street near the Panthéon and right across the street from an apartment once occupied by James Joyce. I took this as a favorable omen. Bert and Jerry, though not expecting me with bag and baggage, were pleased to see that I had accepted their offer. Their place did not disappoint, to say the least. There was a vestibule just inside the front door, with a tiled floor of black and white squares, a coat closet, a brass umbrella stand, and an antique wooden bench with a mirror and brass coat hooks. Beyond that was a living room that dwarfed my parents' entire New York apartment. The ceiling, forty feet above, was bordered with intricate nineteenth-century molding. In the center dangled a huge Tiffany stained glass chandelier. A Persian rug covered most of the 1,000 square feet of polished wood floor. There was a full-sized billiard table, a grand piano, a long buffet table, a sofa, a *chaise longue*, several ornately upholstered armchairs, a well-stocked bar, and gorgeous antique lamps everywhere, ranging from art nouveau to art deco. Forrest green velvet curtains adorned the three tall French windows, all of which opened onto a long balcony with three round patio tables and many potted plants.

Then I got the tour of the large, well-equipped kitchen, the formal dining room, the two full bathrooms, the W.C. (with bidet), and the three beautiful bedrooms. The two that were occupied by Bert and Jerry were appropriately littered with carelessly dropped articles of clothing, and the beds were unmade, but the third one, the one I was to occupy, was pristine with a big double bed, lots of pillows, a heavy bedspread—pale blue, overlaid with densely embroidered white lace. It also had an ornately carved chest of drawers, a matching writing desk, and an armoire. Then there was the study/library with an entire wall of bookshelves and a desk by the window with a gooseneck lamp that was maybe 100 years old.

"H-how did you come by all this?" I stammered, agog.

"Just lucky, I guess," said Jerry with a grin that blended pride with guilt.

It turns out they were both trust fund kids. Their millionaire families were supporting them here, so they could become true men of the world. To Bert and Jerry, that meant throwing lots of parties. No excuse was too small, and my addition to the fold was certainly excuse enough for a grand bash which they planned even as they gave me the tour.

Then they came up with an even better excuse. Charlotte's play would be closing in two weeks—Sunday, October 6th—and they decided to give the cast (especially Charlotte) a big blowout to celebrate a successful run. The last performance would be the matinee, and that would leave plenty of time to get the party started.

Bert and Jerry had party-giving down to a science. We all composed the invitation:

COME ONE, COME ALL—VENEZ TOUS
Bert and Jerry and Jesse (Les Trois Mousquetaires) cordially invite you
to a GRAND FÊTE in honor of the closing of the triumphant engagement of
"Hedda Gabler" at the American Theater starring CHARLOTTE
LIVINGSTON. BRING ONLY YOURSELF. Food and drink will be provided by
the management. Entertainment will be provided by the
DEXTER GORDON QUARTET.

8:00 pm, Dimanche 6 Octobre
60 rue du Cardinal Lemoine
5ème arrondissement, Paris
SOYEZ LÀ OU SOYEZ SQUARE

My big contribution was to find the Dexter Gordon Quartet. That very night, I walked over to the Club Saint-Germain on rue Saint-Benoit, where I knew they were doing an extended engagement. It was right near the Boulevard Saint-Germain. I got there in time to catch the last couple of tunes in the first set. Dexter was in fine form. Surprisingly, when I went up to him, he recognized me from Alexandre's party. Bert and Jerry had commissioned me to offer them 200 francs each to attend with their instruments (I stressed the presence of a Bösendorfer grand piano at the pad). It being a Sunday, they did not have a gig that night, so they all agreed.

Bert and Jerry had a stock list of regulars, who always got invitations. They had them printed up and mailed out from a local printer. They didn't have addresses for Charlotte and her crowd, so they mailed a blanket invitation to her care of the American Theater and gave her carte blanche to invite anyone she chose. The second night after I'd moved in, we all trekked over to le Sélect and found Irving holding court at his usual table. I was feeling expansive and, having no reason to bear him any ill will, gave him and his clique an invitation as well.

They hired the caterer they always used—La Patisserie—they brought people to serve at the buffet table, as well as waiters to pass among the crowd with trays of hors d'oeuvres, and to clean up afterward. I offered to share the expenses, but Bert and Jerry knew I couldn't afford it and turned me down flat.

Over the next two weeks, I had to adjust to living with roommates; roommates whom I had to treat with a certain deference, since I was clearly not regarded as a co-owner, but more of a lodger. My poverty stood in stark contrast to their affluence. I was very careful not to consume food that I did not purchase and to be very fastidious about cleaning up after myself. The study was used exclusively by Bert and Jerry for their writing, and so I set up my typewriter and a lamp on the little desk in my room and continued to scratch away at my novel. I was still determined to finish a longhand draft before starting to type. I no longer took any joy in this process, but now regarded it more as a daunting task that had to be completed, for better or worse.

I also finished *Cat's Cradle* and remained both charmed and intimidated by Vonnegut. I discussed it with Jerry when I returned his book.

"I'm no science fiction writer," I told him, "but I must admit, the whole notion of unintended consequences in science does fascinate me."

"I believe the Earth probably will end someday as a result of some human invention," said Jerry. "Take carbon dioxide, for instance."

"What's carbon dioxide?" I said. "I was never too good at chemistry."

"Carbon dioxide is what comes out of the exhaust pipe of a car. And out of most factory chimneys. You've seen the scene in the old movies where someone commits suicide by locking themselves in the garage with the car motor running? It's lethal. What if the number of cars and factories tripled, and the air got filled with carbon dioxide? Now, trees and plants breathe in carbon dioxide and exhale oxygen. But what if we cut down all the trees to build homes for the growing population?"

"We'd all die from breathing in those fumes," I said. "Wow. That could really happen, huh?"

I got on really well with Jerry. With Bert, things were a bit cooler. I always prided myself on being neat and tidy to the point of fastidiousness, but Bert had me topped. Once, when I hung my unglamorous second-hand overcoat on the coat hook on the mirrored bench in the foyer, he curtly asked me to keep it in my bedroom closet. If I washed a dish or glass and left it in the dish drain for more than fifteen minutes, he would ask me to dry it and put it away in the cupboard. I wondered what I had done to incur his obvious underlying resentment. Every time he walked in on Jerry and I having one of our discussions, he had some excuse to call Jerry into another room. I began to wonder if Bert thought I was supplanting him in Jerry's affections. And I wondered if there were some homosexual undertones to this.

At eight-fifteen Sunday night, the guests began trickling in. At first, a few of the regulars. A group of five of Bert's work friends from the *Tribune*: There were four men and one woman. The woman was with a young girl, about seventeen. She was pale and wispy, with big, sad eyes and a headful of tousled, blondish curls. She was not beautiful, but something about her attracted me. She looked as sad and lonely as I felt. And thin, very thin. I wondered if the older woman was her mother. No introductions were made when Bert greeted them and urged them to help themselves to the buffet. Bert was still giving me the cold shoulder.

Now, more guests began to arrive. So far I knew no one, and no one was introduced to me, so I hung back in a corner and observed the proceedings. There were waiters circulating with trays of cocktails and champagne. I took a glass of champagne, watching the fragile girl with the sad gray eyes. I caught her looking at me once or twice.

The hi-fi was playing mostly jazz records, but all of a sudden a new sound came on. It was a rock record with guys singing in high voices in tight harmonies. The first six songs were not exceptional. Some were covers of R&B records I'd heard before. But the seventh track on Side One, the title track, was exceptional. The melody was infectious and highly original; the lyric, not very deep but practically irresistible. I drifted over to the hi-fi and studied the LP jacket on the top of the stack. The album was called *Please Please Me* by The Beatles. Insects? Oh, I get it—a play on words. Not beet, *beat*. They were four young men with long, shaggy hair— not very different from mine—and from the sleeve notes, I gathered they were English.

"Hey, who put this on?" I yelled, holding up the jacket.

"Hey, baby, wha's happenin'?" came a familiar voice.

It was none other than Tommy Fisk, a denizen of the Village. He was instantly recognizable by his shoulder-length blond hair. No other guy had hair that long. Our paths had crossed many times around Washington Square, although we had never had a full conversation. Now we greeted each other warmly, since neither one of us seemed to know anyone else at the party.

"Tommy Fisk! How'd you get here?"

"Well, it's a long story. See, I had a little hassle with the NYPD. They busted me with a few dozen Black Beauties."

Black Beauties were "A", and "A" was for amphetamine. Tommy was well-known around the Village as an *A-head*. From the manic way he was rattling on, I guessed that hadn't changed.

"So you're still doing that stuff?"

"Yeah." He took a wad of tin foil out of his pocket and unwrapped it, revealing a handful of black capsules. "Want one?"

"No, man," I whispered urgently, "put that away. I *live* here!"

Tommy looked around, as if aware of his surroundings for the first time. "You live *here*?"

"Yeah, and I don't think my roommates would approve. So, where'd you get this record?"

"Oh yeah, so I was sayin', I jumped bail and hopped a freighter for Southhampton. Hung in London for a few weeks. That's where I picked this up. These guys are all the rage there."

"It's really good. I haven't liked rock 'n' roll for a long time, but this shit is different."

"Yeah, *see*! We're ahead of our time. Pretty soon, long hair on guys will be the new in thing!"

"If it is, I'll cut mine short," I quipped.

Meanwhile, the room was filling up with new guests. People of every description and social stratum: the hip and the square, the black and the white. An old hipster came up to the phonograph and ejected the Beatles. "Take that crap off," he said and proceeded to put Dave Brubeck's *Time Out* album on.

"Oh, 'Dave Brubeck Sells Out,'" said Tommy snidely. "You think this is hip? I got news for you, Grandpa, it never was!"

Seeing Tommy hadn't changed his truculent manner, I quietly melted into the crowd. I went looking for the lovely pale, frail girl with the sad eyes. I spotted her over near the piano. She was reading some of the sheet music. This was my entrée. I walked up beside her.

"You play?"

"Comment?"

"Jouez-vous?"

She turned and looked at me and gave me a shy, charming smile. "Ah, oui."

We continued the conversation in French.

"My name is Jesse."

"Kirsten," she said.

We shook hands. "Not very French," I said.

"I'm Danish."

"Your French is very good."

"So is yours."

"But I thought everyone in Scandinavia speaks English."

"We do," she said in English and gave me an enigmatic smile.

I laughed. "Were you testing me?"

"Yes. You passed."

"Kirsten is my protégé," came a voice from behind me. "Soon, all Paris will know her name." It was the tall, older woman she had come in with.

"Are you a pianist as well?" I asked.

"I am Annie d'Arco," she said, looking at me as though she expected me to be impressed.

Quickly taking up the cue, I said, "Oh, Mlle d'Arco! Enchanté! Forgive me for not recognizing you."

She seemed well-satisfied.

"Kirsten, do you think you could play something for us?" Then I whispered in her ear, "Break my heart."

"D'accord," she said with that same enigmatic smile.

I went over to where Tommy and the old jazz hippie were still glowering at each other and unceremoniously lifted the needle from the Brubeck record.

The old guy started to object; I held a finger to my lips. "Shhh. We are about to be serenaded."

As Kirsten took the bench, Mlle d'Arco announced loudly, "Silence, tout le monde, silence s'il vous plaît! Mlle Kirsten Pokrovsky will now play!"

A hush fell over the room. Briefly, she glanced up at me and began to play the most beautiful, heartbreaking piece of music I had ever heard. Of course, I, like everyone else with a scintilla of cultural breeding, recognized it as Debussy's "Au Claire de la Lune." But this was like hearing it for the first time. She poured so much emotion, so much pathos, so much *soul* into it that it did literally break my heart. And suddenly I was in love with the Danish girl with the Russian name playing the French children's song. I desperately wanted to get to know her.

At the end, everyone was silent for a moment, then burst into wild applause. She extended her hand to me, and I gently lifted her from the piano bench.

"Si belle," I whispered. She nodded her head, almost imperceptibly.

From across the room, Jerry was looking at me with an odd expression on his face. Envy?

Mlle d'Arco asked me my name, and suddenly taking me under her wing, she led Kirsten and me back to the group she had come in with and proceeded to introduce me to all of them. Bert had also joined this group, which is why I assumed they were all from the *Tribune*. As it turns out, several of them were, although most were freelancers like Bert. Mlle d'Arco's "date" was none other than Maurice Girodias, the editor and owner of the famed Olympia Press, by far the most innovative and risqué publishing house in Paris, maybe the world. He had been the original publisher of many of the great literary works that had been banned in the U.S. and England: *Lolita*, *The Ginger Man*, *The Story of O*, *Naked Lunch*... I was very anxious to speak with him and make my literary aspirations known to him, but Mlle d'Arco dragged me away to meet more people. Bert regarded me with impotent annoyance as she introduced me around. Somehow I had now incurred the ire of both my roommates.

The main subject of conversation seemed to be the big printers' strike in New York, in which 17,000 union printers had walked off the job at all the major newspapers, crippling the American newspaper industry, including the *New York Herald Tribune*. Everyone was afraid it would affect the Paris edition and they would soon lose their jobs.

There was one striking character who immediately captured my attention. He wore a black patch over his left eye, a black full beard, and a full-length black leather coat.

"And this is Cyclops Lester," said Mlle d'Arco, "He was circulation manager for the *Tribune* until quite recently. Cyclops, this is Jesse."

"Jock Whitney visited, got one look at me, and I was fired on the spot," Cyclops laughed. "Nice to meet you, Jesse. You can call me Cy."

"Jock" Whitney was the owner of the *New York Herald Tribune*, as well as the Paris edition which was now called the international edition. He was the American Ambassador to Great Britain and one of the richest men in America. Very establishment.

The doorbell rang again. Bert opened it and welcomed Dexter Gordon and his band, immediately followed by Irving and two male friends. I heard him introduce them to Bert with not a little pride as Brion Gysin and Harold Norse, "the famous beat poets." I had never heard of them, but my interest was piqued. Irving came over and hugged me warmly. I introduced Kirsten, saying, "You just missed her performance. She's a great concert pianist."

"Oh. Maybe you'll play again for us later," he said. Then he introduced us to Norse and Gysin. I started to ask them about their work, but then Maurice Girodias rushed over and hugged the two poets warmly. He shook hands with Irving, whom he apparently knew only in passing.

"Refugees from the Beat Hotel!" he said.

"What's the Beat Hotel?" I asked.

"Too late, kid. You missed it," said Gysin somewhat snidely.

"I lived there on and off from 1959 until it closed last February," said Norse, who seemed a little more friendly than Gysin. "Brion got there even before me. Ginsberg, Burroughs, Corso... They all lived there on and off." He looked me up and down with a lascivious gleam in his eye.

Irving pulled me aside. "These guys are legendary," he told me sotto voce, "Harold was W.H. Auden's secretary, and he was living with Tennessee Williams when he wrote *The Glass Menagerie*! Between them, they've known—and probably fucked—every major figure in modern literature. The gay ones, of course."

What's with all these gay writers? I wondered. I hoped it wasn't catching. "I suppose you're gonna tell me they're Jewish, too," I joked.

"Norse is! His nom de plume is an anagram of his real name: Rosen."

I rolled my eyes and went to say hello to Dexter, dragging Kirsten along.

"Welcome, and thank you for coming," I said, shaking his hand. Then I introduced Kirsten as a brilliant classical pianist.

"Enchanté mademoiselle," said Dexter in his raspy, ravaged voice, ceremoniously kissing her hand. Then, aside to me: "You got the cash, right? 800 francs."

"Uh, he's the guy with the cash," I said, indicating Bert.

"Go make sure," said Dexter. "I can't cash no check in this town."

I felt uneasy as I approached Bert. "Dexter wanted me to confirm you have the cash for the band. 800 francs."

"Of course I don't have that kind of cash," said Bert. "I'll write him a check."

"I told you they specifically asked for cash," I said.

"You told me?"

"Uh-huh."

"I don't remember you saying that. Well, I don't have it!" Bert's voice was growing increasingly loud.

I made a beeline for Jerry, who was still lurking in the corner, looking sullen.

Kenny Clarke and a guy that worked for him were making trips down to their car and back, bringing in the various drum and trap cases.

"Jerry," I whispered, "we got problems."

After I explained the dilemma, Jerry just looked at me.

"So, what do you want me to do about it? I don't have that much cash."

There was only one thing left to do. I went to my room and got my suitcase down from the closet shelf. I, of course, couldn't have a bank account, so I kept all my money in cash in my suitcase. It was gone. Someone had come into my room—someone at this party—and fleeced me! I eyed Tommy Fisk, who leaned against a wall nearby, looking way too nonchalant.

"Hey Tommy," I said, smiling, "we need 800 francs to pay the band. Could ya lend it to me? Bert can write you a check."

"You kiddin'? I can't cash a check. I'm a wanted man!"

"That's what I thought. Just thought I'd ask." I said cheerfully and gave him an ironically friendly smile.

I decided to consult Kirsten, seemingly my only friend in this place. She was mingling with Mlle d'Arco and Girodias.

"Kirsten, can I talk to you for a minute?" I pulled her aside. "We need to pay the band in cash. 800 francs. Bert was supposed to have it, but he doesn't. Either does Jerry. I went to my room, where I had about 2,500 francs stashed in my suitcase, and I've been cleaned out!"

Kirsten looked alarmed. "You've been robbed?"

"Yes. Here. Tonight. I checked earlier today, and it was all there. Now, nothing."

"Ah, mon cher, that is horrible!"

"Do you think Mlle d'Arco or M. Girodias would have that much cash? Bert could write a check, and I know it's good. These guys are rich. But Dexter needs cash."

Kirsten pulled Mlle d'Arco aside and whispered to her at some length. She nodded.

"Annie has it," said Kirsten.

"Oh, bless you! Bless you, Mlle d'Arco!" I said, grasping both her hands. I went over to Bert.

"Mlle d'Arco will give us the cash if you write her a check," I said.

Bert hesitated for a moment, apparently trying to think of a way to put me in a worse jam. "Okay," he said at last without emotion.

I led Annie d'Arco over to Bert. She produced the cash, he wrote the check. I told Bert to give the cash to Dexter, and he did.

"Merci mille fois," I said to Mlle d'Arco, kissing both her hands.

"Ce n'est rien. Vous êtes un tres gentile garçon." She gave me a sweet smile.

My immediate problem was solved, but I was now flat broke.

At last Charlotte made her entrance with her entourage in tow—all the usual suspects: Meg, Jean-Marc, Brian the Brit, Alexandre, many of the cast members, and more. People clapped and toasted her. She was truly in her element—the toast of the town. Then, something amazing happened. Tommy Fisk walked straight up to Charlotte, took her in his arms, and gave her a big, wet kiss.

Dazed, she smiled up at him. "Tommy! What're you doing here?"

"Hey, baby. Just came to help you celebrate."

I walked over to them. "You know each other?"

"Yeah, man. She's my ol' lady!"

"That's a bit of an overstatement. We were high school sweethearts back home. A million years ago."

"In Stockbridge?"

"Yeah, Stockbridge. You didn't know I was from there, did you, Eddie?"

"No, Tommy, I didn't. And here it's Jesse not Eddie."

"Oh yeah? You undercover too?"

"You might say that. So, that's really amazing." I turned to Charlotte. "I knew Tommy in New York—the Village."

"Well," said Charlotte, "small world."

Dexter and the band started playing "Willow Weep for Me."

"They're playing our song, Ed—er—Jesse."

"Yes, but I have a new dance partner now, 'ma petite char-char.' Besides, I'll bet you two have a lot of catching up to do." Charlotte looked distressed. I went to find Kirsten.

Kirsten and I danced close. It felt good to hold her, but I was, once again, in a world of shit. My roommates both hated me, and I didn't have a centime to my name.

IX

Sunday, 20 Octobre, 1963. Exactly two weeks after the party. One week to the day before my eighteenth birthday.

I awoke next to Kirsten in a luxurious double bed in a deluxe suite in the Hôtel Ritz.

I guess I was just born lucky. What had transpired during and after the party is too much for me to relive now. What's important is that Kirsten and Annie (Mlle d'Arco) gave me shelter at a time when I needed it the most. Annie was independently wealthy and had achieved great success as a concert pianist. She kept a suite at the Ritz, the most luxurious hotel in the world, and Kirsten, her protégé, had her own room there. And I was now Kirsten's lover and constant companion. Kirsten had grown, not only in my affections, but somehow she had also become more beautiful. She made love without inhibitions—what they say about Scandinavian girls is true—and our bodies were a good match.

I had to quit my job at le Sélect because it was now too far from where I was living. I could get there alright taking a couple of busses, but when I got off work at three in the morning, nothing was running, and I couldn't afford to take a cab three nights a week. But Annie saved my ass again. After reading some of my journal-cum-novel, she raved about my writing to her good friend, Maurice Girodias, and he invited me to his office for a meeting. I showed him my handwritten, half-written journal/novel, and he liked it enough to make me an offer.

Maurice had started a subsidiary imprint of the Olympia Press called Ophelia Press, which was dedicated exclusively to pornography. He commissioned me to write pornographic novels—as many and as fast as I could—for a royalty advance of 200 francs for each one I cranked out. I put my novel aside and devoted all my time to writing porn. Hey, I was getting money to write. Porno or no porno, it was a step in the right direction.

Sometimes Kirsten helped me come up with exotic ideas. It's amazing what seventeen-year-old Danish girls know nowadays. The first one was dedicated to the memory of Martisse (although I never used her name). It was an almost-Dickensian story. A young, innocent girl is orphaned at an early age and sent to live with an uncle of dubious moral character. He passes her from man to man for his own profit and amusement. I pictured her getting into all kinds of precarious situations which she could only fuck and suck her way out of. Sometimes she found herself stripped naked and chained to the wall of a dungeon while an evil count whipped her. In the end, she finally finds true love and it all comes out right. I called it *The Erotic Adventures of Annabelle*. I wrote under the pseudonym Terry Malloy, Marlon Brando's character in *On the Waterfront*. These books didn't have to be very long, as long as there was plenty of action on every page.

But the reason I remember that particular Sunday so clearly was the newspaper headline: STABBED BODY RETRIEVED FROM SEINE. It turned out to be Alain. Mme Benoit's kitchen knife was still embedded in his back. The body had washed up somewhere near Rouen, more than seventy miles downstream from Paris. The police were pretty sure he had been the "tueur de prostituées," and they were questioning his mother and everyone who had known any of his victims. A cold wave of fear constricted my insides. I knew that malevolent yenta would sic the police on me if she could. The only reason they hadn't already found me was that practically no one knew I was here. And the Ritz was literally the last place anyone would think to look for me.

I no longer needed to go to work, and I decided it was best not to show my face outdoors, so I just stayed in and wrote. I used the money I'd gotten from Maurice strictly for food. Annie was rehearsing for a concert tour and was gone a lot. Kirsten was also gone most days, attending classes and taking piano lessons at the Conservatoire de Paris, about a twenty-five minute walk away. But she would always bring me food when she returned at the end of the day, usually Chinese or Vietnamese takeout, which was the cheapest. I asked her to also bring me *Le Parisien*, every day. My picture had been in that paper before, and I feared it was just a matter of time before it appeared again.

I was sure they would also question Mme LaBrot. I wondered if she might cast me as a possible suspect to deflect guilt away from herself.

My birthday came and went. Happy birthday to me. I told no one, not even Kirsten. And then it happened: POLICE SEEK TEENAGE BOY IN CONNECTION WITH SLAYING OF HOOKER KILLER. And there I was. The same picture my parents had sent to the American embassy last summer. The same one the cops had. The same one that had been in that very paper. The photo was a year old when they sent it, and I looked very different even then. Now, no one would be able to recognize me from that lousy snapshot. That was good. But it gave both my real name and pseudonym: "Edward Strull aka Jesse Bright." And that was bad.

Of course, when Kirsten saw it, I had to tell her the whole story. Well, not quite all of it. I told her about my relationship with Martisse, how I had been the Benoits' boarder, and how I suspected Alain had been the "tueur de prostituées." I left out the part where I set him up to be murdered by Mme LaBrot's henchmen. I assured her I didn't kill him, though I wanted to, and she believed me. She said she would stand by me no matter what.

But then, a few days later, Kirsten announced that she would be going on tour with the Young People's Symphony of the Conservatoire de Paris, and then home to Copenhagen for Christmas. She was very excited and happy, and I tried to be happy for her. But I was dying inside. With both Kirsten and Annie gone, I would be left alone to fend for myself.

Kirsten suggested I go along with her on the tour and then to Copenhagen to meet her family. I pointed out that the police were looking for me and that they had both my real name and alias. But Kirsten was not deterred. "The orchestra has eighty members. We will take two large busses, plus a big truck for the larger instruments. I'm the only one that will not need to bring my instrument." She had my attention.

"So?"

"So, how about if I get you a job as one of the instrument carriers? You and three other guys carry and help set up at each concert. Can you drive a truck?"

"I can't drive anything."

"That's okay. I'll tell them you'll work cheap."

"But how am I supposed to get across all those international borders?"

"That's the beauty of it. We will have so many people, they won't be able to scrutinize everyone. Do you think they'll check every name and photo of eighty-five people?"

"You know, it just might work," I said. "You, my darling, are a genius!" I kissed her passionately. What did I do to deserve a girl like this?

She smiled. "We leave in a week."

I used that week to finish a second draft of *The Erotic Adventures of Annabelle*, proofread it five times, and send it off to Maurice. In the cover letter, I asked Maurice to address all correspondence to Terry Malloy c/o Annie d'Arco, Suite 450, Hôtel Ritz and explained I would be out of town for a while but mail would be forwarded to me.

I decided to use the forged British passport, so my name was still Jesse Bright when I reported to M. Christophe, the tour manager, at the Conservatoire early on the morning of November eleventh. The big moving truck was parked outside. I wore my second-hand overcoat, my prop eyeglasses, and a black worker's cap. Kirsten confirmed that I looked nothing like the photo in the paper. I never spoke to the conductor, M. Gallois-Montbrun, but he was the boss of everyone. The road crew consisted of me and three much bigger, stronger guys: Étienne, Bernard, and a huge Russian named Tolya. They all ribbed me about my diminutive size and lack of physical strength.

"How did *you* get this job?" Bernard cracked, smiling good-naturedly.

I just smiled and said, "Connections."

Nevertheless, I resolved to work my ass off to show them that I was going to pull my weight and then some. Our first job was to load in all the large instruments, which were waiting for us in hardshell cases on the stage of the school auditorium. Étienne, who had done last year's tour, directed us. There was a precise order in which the instruments had to be packed. The biggest pieces went in first: tympani, bass viols, a big rectangular case I was told contained a marimba, a harp, a trap case containing a snare drum and various percussion instruments. Next came the smaller stuff: celli and things like trombones, bassoons, and French horns. All of the instruments had to be secured in place with ropes that were tied to metal bars affixed to the inner walls of the truck. The violins, violas, flutes, and trumpets were allowed to stay with their owners on the busses.

I took off my overcoat and started hauling the heavy cases. Most of them had wheels, but getting them down from the stage, then down the front steps of the school, and then up into the truck was the hard part; it usually took two of us for that. I worked up a sweat very quickly, even in the cold November air. As each row of instruments was loaded in, we inserted large pieces of foam rubber between them to ensure they would not roll around and bump into each other.

Then there were ten wardrobe trunks containing the musicians' concert attire—tuxes for the men, floor-length gowns for the women. There was one trunk labeled simply KIRSTEN POKROVSKY. *She gets an entire trunk for herself?*

There was only room in the front seat of the truck for the three big guys. I was consigned to "the dungeon," the pitch-dark, windowless cargo section where all the instruments were stowed. You'd think one of the big guys would go back there, making it more comfortable for three of us to sit in the front seat with my skinny ass taking up so little space, but no. I got to take a battery-powered lantern, a book (I was now reading a wonderful collection of short stories by Robert W. Chambers called *The King in Yellow*, horror and science fiction written in the late nineteenth century), and my novel/memoir, which had now grown to four spiral notebooks. I also took a pee bucket, just in case...

The tour would last two weeks. Our first stop would be within France: the Auditorium-Orchestre National de Lyon. It was a grand and elegant hall. As we trudged back and forth lugging the instrument cases, I was awestruck by the size and majesty of the place. The thought of my Kirsten playing here filled my heart with pride.

But it wasn't until the actual concert that I got the full import of what was happening. First, three short orchestral pieces. No Kirsten. Then, the finale of Part One. A hush fell over the packed house. Then Kirsten appeared, resplendent in a sparkling blue evening gown. She walked regally to the piano to thunderous applause. Kirsten was the star of the whole thing! No wonder she was able to get me hired, no questions asked.

She played magnificently—Brahms' "Piano Concerto No. 1." I'm far from a classical music aficionado, but I must admit the music swept me away, crashed over me in waves. She got a standing ovation, bowed graciously to the conductor and the audience, received two large bouquets, and exited.

Backstage, she planted a big kiss on my lips in front of everyone. I was speechless. I had no idea what a big deal she was. What must the others have thought? She could have had any man in the place and she kissed a ragamuffin! I felt my face heat up. I must've turned red as a boiled lobster.

After the intermission, the orchestra played a few more numbers, then the grand finale: Kirsten playing Ravel's "Piano Concerto in G Major." The audience went wild. They loved her—and so did I.

A group of admirers and music critics wanted her to come to a big party, but Kirsten shyly demurred, saying we had to get up early and travel to our next destination.

My fellow crew members now regarded me with new respect.

"'Connections,' huh?" said Étienne sarcastically. "I'll say."

While the orchestra was wined and dined at a nice restaurant, Bernard, Étienne, Tolya, and I worked for two more hours, packing the instruments into their cases and the cases into the truck. Finally, someone brought us coffee and sandwiches. They put us up for the night in a large, commercial hotel. Everyone had to share a room with a member of the same sex, so I couldn't sleep with Kirsten. I roomed with Tolya, the Russian bear.

Fortunately, we didn't have to get up at the crack of dawn. Our next stop, Geneva, was only 150 kilometers away, about an hour and a half's drive. I was nervous; this would be our first crossing of an international border. I had heard the Swiss were quite lax about these things and I hoped it was true.

Nevertheless, when we got to the border, we all had to get out of the busses and the truck and line up to have our passports stamped by the Swiss authorities. It was chilly, so there was nothing odd about my wearing my cap and overcoat and putting the collar up. The customs men were much more interested in looking at the truck's cargo and we had to open several of the instrument cases for them. The man with the rubber stamp gave each of us a cursory glance and then stamped our passports. He made a check mark on a list he carried with all of our names. I breathed a sigh of relief. One down and five more borders to cross.

The venue in Geneva was the magnificent Victoria Hall, with its gilded rococo walls and an imposing pipe organ, dead center, looming over the orchestra. We set about immediately loading the instruments into the hall. Every instrument case had the name of its player stenciled on with white spray paint. We had to memorize where each different cello player sat, as well as each French horn, bass viol, bassoon, etc., etc. We also labeled the seat of each chair with a musician's last name, using masking tape.

The program—and the response—was exactly the same in Geneva as it had been in Lyon. The Lyon papers carried glowing reviews of the orchestra and especially of Kirsten. Backstage after the show, she was, once again, mobbed with admirers, journalists, and photographers. My Kirsten was becoming an overnight sensation. Now, there could be no more stolen kisses in the wings. Now, for both our sakes, I had to keep my distance. Every so often, I would catch her staring longingly in my direction. I just had to shrug and stare back helplessly.

Our next stop was Milan, an Italian city I had not visited on my camping trip. But there would be no sightseeing on this trip. I endured some nerve-wracking scrutiny crossing the border, but at last they stamped my forged British passport and let me through. All the visas I was collecting enhanced the credibility of this passport.

At the hotel in Milan, there was a letter waiting for me (addressed to Jesse Bright, Orchestre de Conservatoire de Paris, Hôtel Cristoforo Colombo, Milano, Italia), with no return address. I opened it when I got to my room. Inside was the picture of me clipped from *Le Parisien* with a note in French that read: "We know where you are. Do not talk no matter what." It was unsigned, but I knew it had come from Mme LaBrot and her henchmen. The Paris cops must be putting the squeeze on them. I burned the letter in the wastebasket and opened the window to let the smoke out before Tolya came in. If they were trying to scare me, they were doing a damn fine job. I wondered if Albert and Aziz would be waiting for me around some corner to cut my throat.

The drive to Salzberg, Austria took fifteen hours and involved two border crossings, which took forever: from Italy to Germany, from Germany to Austria. By the time we reached Salzberg, we were all exhausted. We ate and checked into our hotel and slept. The concert was the next evening. M. Christophe had planned everything meticulously and booked all the hotels months in advance. In Salzberg, our party occupied the entire place.

Kirsten's picture was in all the local papers. That night's show was standing room only. All our concerts were now sold out and they added a new one: the Opéra de Paris in the opulent Palais Garnier. The Conservatoire's own concert hall, le Salle des Concerts, was too small, only 1,000 seats.

There was no way I was going to try to re-enter France now. After the Salzberg concert, I pulled Kirsten aside.

"I'm going to disappear after Brussels," I said. "I'll tell M. Christophe I have a family emergency in London. That way, maybe I can collect my paycheck. I'll meet you in Copenhagen."

"Take the train to Amsterdam," she said. "You can wait for me there."

She gave me the name of the Hotel Sphinx, a cheap hotel in Amsterdam, and a check from Maurice made out to me for 200 francs. There was a note from him, asking for another installment of *The Erotic Adventures of Annabelle*. "Annie sent this. She saw your picture in the newspaper and told me to stay away from you." She smiled that magical smile of hers. "But I won't. The Paris concert is on the twenty-third. I'll write you at the Sphinx and tell you when I'll be arriving." She stuffed another hundred francs into my pocket. "This should keep you going until I get there." We started to kiss but looked around and thought better of it.

X	Brussels, November 22nd, 1963. It was about eight o'clock Friday night. I was on my way to the Central Station to catch my train to Amsterdam, suitcase in my hand, knapsack on my back, when I passed a crowd of silent people clustered around the window of an appliance shop. Some were crying. In the window, a TV was showing the news. John F. Kennedy, President of the United States, had been shot in Dallas, Texas—in the head, and it was uncertain whether or not he would survive.

Like everyone, I was stunned. How could something like this happen in *my country*? Suddenly, I felt very American. JFK was the first president in my lifetime with whom I identified, whom I cared about. His administration, which began the year I started high school, marked a new era in American politics. We were all pulling for him. He was loved and admired by everyone in the world, it seemed. Apparently not everyone.

At one a.m., I was on the train. At a stop about halfway to the Netherlands border, a man came through the car, selling newspapers in Dutch, of which I could make neither heads nor tails. There was a photo of JFK on the front page, and I gathered from the gasps and cries of the other passengers that he was dead. The grief seemed contagious, and I felt my eyes tearing up. I was bonding with my fellow travelers by grieving with them, and at the same time I felt very alone. I was now completely on my own again. I missed Kirsten terribly. She always had the answers; she always had a plan. Now, I was rudderless.

I decided to write another letter to my parents. I still had an unused light-blue onionskin *par avion* envelope with postage and matching stationery. It occurred to me that I had never checked for mail at the American Express office. There were probably multiple letters from them, sitting there, waiting for me. I decided not to mention this.

Dear Mom & Dad,

Sorry I haven't been in touch. I have been busy writing and working at a café. Then I went on tour with a symphony orchestra. I sold a novella to a French publisher. I just learned about JFK. Am desolate! What kind of a country are you living in anyway? As you can tell from the postmark and stamps, I am in the Netherlands. Long story short, I'm on a short vacation with my girlfriend, who is a piano prodigy at the Conservatoire de Paris. She is my age and quite lovely in every way. As you know, I am now 18, but I cannot reveal my exact location as yet. It's complicated. Suffice it to say, I will have some interesting stories to tell when next I see you. Don't worry, I will be alright. My love to Janey.

Love,

Eddie

I'll mail this from Amsterdam. I'm not sure it will be much of a comfort to them.

They didn't make us get off the train at the Dutch border. A uniformed agent went through the cars, examining and stamping passports. He did a cursory examination of my suitcase and knapsack, did not find my U.S. passport because of the false bottom I had installed, stamped my fake passport, and moved on.

When I got off the train at Amsterdam's Central Station at four in the morning (every city in Europe, it seems, has a Central Station), it was snowing. It was damn cold. I buttoned my old overcoat all the way up and wrapped my used woolen muffler tight around my neck. There were a couple of taxis outside the station, and I took one to the Hotel Sphinx at Weteringschans 82. Luckily, I had the foresight to change all of my French francs into Dutch guilders after buying my train ticket in Brussels. I had also phoned the Sphinx and reserved the cheapest single room they had.

The night clerk was a blond young man, about my age, probably a college student. I apologized about waking him and gave him my name—Jesse Bright—for the reservation. I also had to surrender my passport. He picked up my bag and sleepily ushered me into a rickety elevator, to the fourth floor, and down a musty, carpeted corridor to room 406.

The room overlooked the street, and thankfully, the radiator was pumping out plenty of steam heat. Other than that, the drab little room had a cot, a table, a chest of drawers, a closet, and a chair. Adequate for my needs. I thanked the clerk, saying "Dank je," two of the five words in Dutch I remembered, and tipped him a guilder. He seemed surprised (it was worth maybe a half-dollar) and said, "Thank *you*, sir!" in perfect English.

"I'll be needing a room with a larger bed when my girlfriend gets here."

"And when will that be?"

"I'm not quite sure," I said. "Maybe a few days. Maybe a week."

"Okay. We will see what we can do."

The bed was narrow but clean (Holland is nothing if not clean) and, as I had been up for eighteen hours, I had no trouble falling asleep.

The first thing I did the next day was write a letter to Kirsten:

> *My Darling,*
> *Just arrived at the Sphinx and already I am missing you like crazy. When will you be here? I need you! Write to me as Jesse Bright.*
> *All my love,*
> *E*

Unfortunately, my salary for the tour was not immediately available. M. Christophe assured me that a check would be mailed to me in due course, care of Kirsten. I knew I would run out of money very soon, so I immediately set about writing *The Further Erotic Adventures of Annabelle*. In this installment, Annabelle escapes from the S&M dungeon of the evil Count Malvois and stows away on a Spanish frigate heading for the West Indies (this takes place in 1872). Unluckily, the Captain and crew turn out to be a bunch of kinky, perverted pirates and when the lovely Annabelle is discovered hiding in the cargo hold…well, you can guess the rest. Having read several of the other pornographic novellas on Maurice's Ophelia imprint, I knew the book didn't have to have much literary merit, as long as there was plenty of sex. So, I wrote as quickly as I could. Right now, Maurice was my best chance of getting enough money to survive a while longer.

Days went by, with no word from Kirsten. I spent all day every day writing. The frigid weather outside provided further inducement for me to remain indoors with my nose to the grindstone.

I became friendly with Ricard, the night clerk. It turned out he too was a writer. He wrote in English, and we agreed to proofread each other's work. More days went by. Ricard, knowing my plight, smuggled me buttered toast with chocolate and tea to keep me going. It was Thanksgiving in the States and my hunger and loneliness made me miss home even more.

A week had gone by and still no word from Kirsten. Then, a package came. In it was a copy of my slim volume, *The Erotic Adventures of Annabelle*, and an envelope from Maurice containing another fifty francs. I, at last, held in my hand my first published work. The irony of the fact that it was under a pseudo-pseudonym and I could never tell anyone about it was not lost on me. Maurice told me the book was selling moderately well, mainly at the Librairie Anglaise, an English-language bookshop on the Left Bank, and the money was my first royalty installment.

That was the good news. The bad news waited for me in another envelope from Annie d'Arco.

> *Mon Cher Jesse—or Eddie (which is it?),*
>
> *I regret to inform you that, as Kirsten's guardian, I cannot allow any further communication between the two of you. I have withheld from her the letters you have sent. Similarly, I did not mail the one letter she wrote to you. Right now, her career as a pianist is taking off like a rocket. She is constantly hounded by journalists for interviews. Your name and likeness have appeared in several newspapers lately. Being publicly associated with a man wanted by the police would be a devastating scandal for her. I believe I have made her understand this, and she has promised me she will never see you again.*
>
> *I am still fond of you, Jesse, and I wish only the best for you. If you ever get yourself out of this mess, perhaps we can all be friends again. Bon chance!*
> *Annie*

I was crushed. The air went out of my lungs, the blood drained from my face. I collapsed on my bed. I didn't think I could ever recover from this blow. All my hopes for a brighter future, all my dreams of being with Kirsten forever were now dashed.

Unless I went back to Paris and made a clean breast of it. After all, what did they have on me? A forged passport. They would try to make me give up the name of the forger. I'll refuse. Can they put me in jail for that? They will try to make me tell what I know about Alain's murder. I'll say I know nothing. I needed legal advice. Free legal advice. I decided to write to Maurice.

> Dear Maurice,
>
> Merci mille fois for the check and the book. From now on, please write to me directly as Jesse Bright, Hotel Sphinx, Weteringschans 82, Rm. 406, Amsterdam, Netherlands.
>
> If you've seen the papers, you know I'm a wanted man in France. I want to return to Paris and clear my name. I need legal advice. All my money was stolen at the party the night we met, so I am broke. Can you recommend a pro bono criminal attorney?
>
> Thanks in advance for all your help,
> Jesse

There was another option: I could present myself at the American Embassy in Amsterdam, tell them my passport and money had been stolen, and get them to contact my parents and send me back to the States. No. Too humiliating. I was determined to fix this mess myself.

All my life, all I wanted was to be an adult, to take responsibility for my own life. Now that I finally was one, it was time to walk the walk. I mailed the letter to Maurice and tried to keep writing the Annabelle sequel with a heart full of dread.

XI

A week passed. I wrote every day and tried like hell not to think about Kirsten. It was now December and the weather outside was even colder. Ricard kept me alive with tea and toast. He told me they were ice skating on the canals and asked if I wanted to go. He would lend me a pair of skates. I was a pretty fair ice skater at one time, but I declined. I needed to get the Annabelle sequel finished and off to Maurice. I was also waiting for his reply to my plea for legal help. Finally, I got a letter from him:

"…I do know one or two attorneys who might help you, but it is almost Christmas and no one will be in their office until after the first of the year…"

Almost Christmas. Kirsten would be in Copenhagen. I thought about going there and trying to find her, but the train fare would eat up all my money. Maybe I could call her parents' house. I asked Ricard where I could get a Copenhagen phonebook. He directed me to the nearest public library.

I walked the slippery, cobbled five blocks and froze my ass off. Christmas lights and decorations adorned the shops and were strung between the ancient lampposts. Christmas shoppers bustled from shop to shop. As I passed over the canal, the skaters were out in force. I paused to watch for a moment, remembering my days as a kid ice skating in Central Park's Wollman Memorial or at Radio City. My ears were painfully cold. I passed a used clothing shop and thought about buying a hat with earflaps. I actually saw one and tried it on. It was one of those red-and-black checked hunter's hats, probably from the forties or fifties, but it looked so stupid on me, I decided against it. I felt a kind of visceral negativity about it. Was it the idea of hunting? Or maybe something I'd read somewhere.

Besides, I wasn't about to give up my old, black worker's cap with the snap on the brim.

It was nice and warm inside the library. I asked a librarian if they had a Copenhagen phone book, and they did. How many Pokrovskys could there be? There were forty-three. How could there be so many Russians in Denmark? I went to the Reference section and opened the World Atlas. Now I could see why: Copenhagen was just across the Baltic Sea from the West Coast of the Soviet Union, and even closer to Poland. It was hopeless. I couldn't even afford to call all those Pokrovskys. And what if her family lived in a suburb that wasn't even part of the Copenhagen phonebook?

Crestfallen, I returned to my tiny room. I now had only one viable course of action: to wait until Maurice got me a lawyer—after the New Year—return to Paris and face the music. Waiting was never one of my strong suits.

Anyway, Annie might have been right. Being with me might damage Kirsten's rising career, and I would sooner die than hurt her.

I returned to the Annabelle sequel. In my mind, she looked like Martisse. I was writing all this degenerate filth, and it was turning me on. I wrote half the book with a boner, but it drove me to write with more passion. It had an emotionally upbeat ending, as Annabelle was at last rescued by a young, handsome nobleman who treated her with kindness and respect in spite of her checkered past and who genuinely loved her. The love they made was the first she had ever experienced that was truly satisfying, both physically and emotionally. Upon finishing, I felt this book was far better than the first slap-dash Anabelle book. I proofread it several times and typed it up on the typewriter Ricard had lent me, making revisions as I went. Proudly, I sent the finished product off to Maurice with a note saying I thought this was the best work I had done yet, porno or not, and that I hoped he would feel the same. I added that I was anxiously waiting for after the New Year, when I would get that introduction to a lawyer. Then, I hit him up for another 200-franc advance.

New Year's Eve, 1963. Ricard had invited me to a party, which promised to be a wild one. I felt I had earned a bit of R&R, since I had finished another book. It was at the home of one of his fellow students at the University of Amsterdam. I was ready to drown my sorrows in beer and vodka and perhaps a buxom blond Dutch damsel. I had passed many on the street I wouldn't kick out of bed.

It turns out Ricard's friend Stefan and his two roommates occupied three floors in one of those elegant seventeenth-century gabled houses. It overlooked a wide canal, whose name I can neither remember nor pronounce. But it was a beautiful party pad.

We had picked up a bottle of decent vodka on the way over, so we did not arrive empty-handed. The party was well underway. We showed up fashionably late, since we both agreed that spending hours milling about at a party grew tedious fast. The pungent smell of burning hashish was the first thing that hit me. Smoking hash was one of the major pastimes of Amsterdam's youth. They were playing that Beatles album. I made a mental note to buy a copy when I got some money. There were also singles by two more English rock bands: The Hollies, who had really good vocal harmonies like the Beatles, and The Rolling Stones, who were more bluesy and who covered what I found out was a Beatles song, "I Wanna Be Your Man." The Amsterdam crowd seemed to favor rock 'n' roll and rhythm & blues over jazz.

A pretty girl gave me a hit off a pipe. She was not blonde, but buxom. We flashed on each other immediately. Her name was Kristina, and she was a fast-mover. After five minutes of small talk, we were in a coat closet, making out, groping under each other's clothing. We were only prevented from getting naked on the spot by one of the guests, who needed his coat. I turned and saw who it was: Art Rosen!

Of course, why didn't I think of it? The University of Amsterdam. That's where he taught. But still, this was a terribly unnerving coincidence.

"Eddie?"

"Hi, Art. H-how are you?"

"You really did a number on me, Eddie. The camp will never hire me again, I nearly lost my job at the university—and your parents. I certainly caught an earful from them. You caused all of us so much trouble, so much *anguish*. Did you even *think* what you were doing?"

His voice was rising. His face was getting red. Kristina put herself together and fled. Art continued his rant:

"Do you ever think how your actions affect other people? Do you even give a damn?"

"I'm sorry, Art. Truly sorry. I didn't want to hurt anybody."

"Well, you did! I still get letters from your parents. They said you wrote to them from Paris—once."

"I wrote again on the way up here…"

"What do you want, a medal? Are you ever going home?"

"I don't know. I'm eighteen now, you know."

"So that makes it alright? Ruining people's lives?"

"I never thought of it like that."

"You never thought at all. What are you doing in Amsterdam anyway?"

"It's a long story. I've been writing. My second book is about to be published." I said this with a stupid little smile on my face, as if this bit of news would somehow make him proud of me.

"I don't give a damn if you wrote *War and Peace*. You're the most selfish, thoughtless kid I've ever known."

And with that, he put on his coat and gloves and walked out the door.

I searched the room for Ricard and found him enmeshed in a passionate debate with two guys about who killed Kennedy. Was it the KKK? The Communists? The Mob? No one thought it was one man acting alone.

I was visibly shaking.

"Jesse, what's wrong?"

"What happened to that vodka?" I asked.

"Over there," he said, pointing to a table laden with libations.

I poured myself three fingers and downed it.

"I'm sorry, Ricard, I gotta go."

"What? Why? I thought you and that girl…"

"I'll explain later. Happy New Year."

"Happy New Year," he said, looking forlorn and puzzled.

I got my hat and coat and trudged back to the hotel, immersed in thought. All around me, the streets were swarming with people shouting "Happy New Year" in Dutch and other languages, blowing noisemakers, wearing silly hats. I was barely aware of them. Somehow I wound up at my hotel. I couldn't even say how I got there.

Art's ire haunted me. I thought about calling my parents collect but decided instead to write them a long, heartfelt letter, apologizing again and telling them where I was. I told them to write to me as Jesse Bright, that I was going under my pen name with no further explanation.

On January second, I got Maurice's response to my manuscript:

> *27 decembre, 1963*
> *Dear Jesse,*
>
> *I liked the first Annabelle book better. Although the writing is better here, it's too nice. Too soft. We're after rough sex, S&M, torture. That's what our readers expect. I will publish this, but without much hope for a good return. Enclosed is another advance of 200 francs. The first Annabelle book is selling well and you will get a full accounting twice a year: in February and August. The February statement will be forthcoming in about three weeks and may yield a few more francs for you.*
>
> *I will be calling lawyers on your behalf starting 2 janvier.*
> *I will keep you posted.*
>
> *With kind regards,*
> *Maurice*

I decided I couldn't write that rough, nasty stuff Maurice was asking for. It was just not in my nature. Every time I wrote about a girl—even though she was imaginary—I couldn't help but fall in love with her. And my love was always soft and gentle. So now, I turned my attention back to my novel, which is what my journal had become. I had now filled eight spiral notebooks. The encounter with Art had to be in there somehow. Too dramatic to pass up. Having him discover me in a closet with a girl was also too good to change. Sometimes you can't top reality. Anyway, it gave me something to do while I waited.

XII As before, I mostly stayed in my room. I stayed up writing 'til all hours of the night. The overactive radiator and a hot water pipe that ran right through my room, close to the ceiling, made my room stifling—too hot to sleep. I would open the window for short periods, but then it would get too cold. During the day, I could open the window and get under the covers, so I slept then, except when the maids kicked me out to clean the room and change the bedding. This also fit in with Ricard's working hours. He was the only other person I interacted with. He continued to filch food and bring it to me and he was able to cash Maurice's checks into guilders, which I used to pay the rent. I was eternally in his debt, and I told him so.

I had a long talk with him about the altercation with Art at the party. I confessed how guilty I was feeling. Art had been right; he'd made me see how selfish and myopic I had been. Ricard tried to assuage my guilt by telling me that rebellion was a normal part of growing up, and the fact that I saw it differently now showed that I had grown up.

The novel was beginning to take shape. Essentially, it reflected my travails in Europe but included musings about the emotional damage I had inflicted on others (Art, my family, Robin). It was a story of coming of age in which a willful, rebellious teen starts to think outside his own selfish desires and learns to care about the feelings of others. When I started fictionalizing my story, I thought the fierce independence of my protagonist would make him a hero; now he was becoming something less—maybe not the villain of the piece, but certainly terribly flawed.

At last, the letter I had been waiting for from Maurice arrived:

Dear Jesse,

An attorney friend of mine has agreed to take on your case pro bono. His name is André Berenwald. His office is at 63 Avenue Jean Jaurès, arrondissement 19. His telephone number is 33-Macmahon-91-73. He is fluent in English as well as French. He asks that you telephone his office and set up an appointment to come and see him. Do NOT write to him. He wants no paper record of your case until he has had a chance to speak with you. Do this as soon as you get this letter. Time is of the essence. Have you seen the latest French papers? You are being portrayed as the 'Number One Suspect' in the murder of Alain Benoit. This is serious, mon amie. Enclosed is another 100 francs to cover your train fare. If you are arrested at the border, call the number I have given you immediately. Say nothing to the police until André gets there. I look forward to seeing you in Paris very soon. Bon chance!

Maurice

P.S. I liked 'The Further Erotic Adventures of Annabelle' better upon second reading.

"Number One Suspect!" Now I regretted running away. Running away from Paris, running away from America, running away from my family. Now I saw that one solves nothing by running away. It just makes you look guilty. I didn't know what awaited me back in France, but I was through running away. And I wasn't going to rat out Mme LaBrot. After all, I was the one who put her up to it. I had killed him, just as surely as if I'd had the guts to plunge the knife into his back myself.

When I thought about it, they really had nothing on me except the phony passport, and if I destroyed that, there was no concrete evidence it ever existed. If I got rid of that and just kept my mouth shut, they had no proof of anything. Maybe they would deport me back to the U.S., and maybe that would not be such a bad thing. Now, I was anxious to check out of the

Hotel Sphinx and catch that train back to Paris. I was ready to face my fate, whatever it might be.

I waited until eight p.m. when Ricard came on duty, so I could say goodbye to him. When he arrived, I was waiting in the lobby, all bundled up for the freezing walk, and bags packed. I got my forged British passport back and burned it in the loo. Ricard looked puzzled, but didn't say anything about it.

"Jesse, you're leaving?"

"Yes. I'm afraid I have to. Urgent business in Paris. Someday, I'll tell you all about it. I wanted to thank you again for all your kindness."

"Don't mention it."

"Too late; I just did."

"Ha ha! Always with the jokes."

"Am I all paid up?"

"Ja. To the end of the week. You have some change coming." He plunked a few guilders down on the counter.

"I'll write to you—and send you a copy of my book, if it ever gets published."

"Don't wait for that. Send me a manuscript."

"Oh yes. I might get a letter from my parents in New York. Their name is Strull. Could you forward it to me at this address?" And I wrote down Maurice's office address.

"No problem."

"Okay. Vaarwell, Ricard."

"Vaarwell, Jesse."

Once I got outside, I decided to splurge on a cab.

At the station, I bought a one-way ticket (second class) on the 10:15 to Paris. While I waited, I took out Maurice's letter, copied the lawyer's info onto a small piece of paper, and put it in my inside breast pocket with my U.S. passport. Then I burned the letter in an ashtray. Then I remembered the other letters from Maurice concerning getting me a lawyer. I rummaged in my knapsack and found them. I burned those, too. The last thing I wanted was to drag Maurice into this.

I couldn't write, I couldn't read, I couldn't sleep. All the way to the French border, I was plagued by visions of being dragged off the train by gendarmes and taken in chains to a Paris jail. I decided to write a letter to Annie:

> *Ma chère Annie,*
>
> *I am writing to tell you that I have abided by your advice to stay away from Kirsten. I am now on my way back to Paris to give myself up to the police and clear my name, since I am guilty of nothing. By the time you read this, it is likely I will be in a French jail. Our mutual friend, whom I will not name here, found me a lawyer. If you want to write to me, do it care of him.*
>
> *Please tell Kirsten I think of her constantly, but for now, it is better for us not to be in touch. Tell her I count the minutes until I am completely exonerated and can see her again (if she still wants to).*
>
> *Joyeux Noël et bonne année,*
> *Jesse/Eddie*

I encountered no trouble passing over the German and then Belgian border. We traveled through the night and into the morning, mostly through Germany. I posted the letter in Brussels, where I had to change trains. I hadn't eaten in a long time, so I bought a small packet of peanuts from a vending machine. They were stale. After eating a few, I rolled up the cellophane bag and put it in my pocket. Time to board my train.

Getting ever closer to the French border, my anxiety rose. When the train stopped at the French border, near Lille, the customs men came through the cars, stamping passports, I saw them checking the passengers' names against a list. *Here it comes*, I thought, *here it comes*. And it did come.

After taking my passport, the guard was giving me the fish eye, looking at the photo in the passport, looking at his list, then down at me.

"You are Edward Strull, also known as Jesse Bright?" the guard said to me.

"À vôtre service," I said, standing up and dramatically offering my hands in front of me to be cuffed.

The guards all laughed. "Ce n'est pas nécessaire," said my guy, and he led me gently by the elbow off the train and into a police car. Another gendarme grabbed my suitcase and knapsack.

They took me to the local police station at Lille, where I was placed in a holding cell with a drunk who was passed out on the only bench, wreaking of piss. The arresting officer got the Chief Inspector and showed me to him. Then they went to a phone and called—presumably—the man in charge of the Alain Benoit homicide investigation. About four hours went by. They gave me coffee and a very nice sandwich of liverwurst on a baguette. French jail food was better than most American school food. Anyway, I was starving at this point, so I couldn't be much of a judge. I was able to eat it all, in spite of my cellmate's aroma. Finally, a plainclothes inspector and two uniformed Paris cops, replete with capes, showed up, put me and my stuff in a car, and drove me toward Paris.

The inspector introduced himself as Chief Inspector Juno Paletti. I was handcuffed and seated in the back with one of the gendarmes. The inspector sat in the front passenger seat and eyed me in the rearview mirror. The other gendarme drove.

"So," he said, "you are the famous Jesse Bright."

"Je m'appelle Edward Strull," I said, remaining expressionless.

He opened my passport and the small piece of paper with my lawyer's info dropped out.

"So it says here," he said, examining my passport and ignoring the piece of paper, "but don't you also call yourself Jesse Bright?"

"My lawyer's information is on that piece of paper that just dropped into your lap. Please don't lose it. I can say nothing more until he is present."

"Comme vous voulez, monsieur," he said.

Throughout the rest of the trip, the cops kept up a steady banter in French, as if they thought I couldn't understand, which went something like:

"Somebody's schooled this little punk quite well."

"Don't worry. He won't be so brave after a few hours in 'le trou.'"

Le trou. The hole? What the hell is that?

"I hope he likes our rats." They all laughed.

As cold as it was, I began to sweat.

"Am I under arrest?" I asked in English.

"Non, mon petit," said the inspector, "you are just wanted for questioning."

I gathered they thought to soften me up in "the hole" for a few hours before the interrogation.

They drove me to the main police headquarters building at 36 quai des Orfèvres. It was a stone's throw from Nôtre Dame on the Île de Cité. Good old "Boul'Miche" ran right by it.

Before they had a chance to throw me in the hole, I said in French:

"Before you lock me up, I insist on calling my lawyer. It is my right, no?" and I held out my hand for the piece of paper the inspector was holding.

"Yes, it is your right," said the inspector, and he handed me my piece of paper and escorted me to a payphone in the long corridor which reminded me of my public elementary school, with walls painted glossy pale green and the hard, black-and-white linoleum floor that reverberated with every footstep. I had just enough change to call M. Berenwald. I got his secretary on the line. She said he was with a client and asked for my number.

"Just tell him it's Jesse Bright, aka Edward Strull, Maurice Girodias' friend. Tell him I'm at police headquarters at 36 quai des Orfèvres and to please come at once. They are going to put me in solitary confinement and then interrogate me. Tell him to refer to me as Edward Strull. That's Edward S-T-R-U-L-L. Do you have all that?"

"Yes," she said, "I wrote it all down."

I said, "Merci" and hung up.

"Take him down," said the inspector, and the two gendarmes took me by my arms and led/dragged me into a stairwell and down, and down, and down. We emerged in an ancient basement dungeon, complete with oozing stone walls and tiny windowless cells. They threw me into one of them. I did not see any other prisoners around. It was cold and dank and very dark. For the first time, I was really scared. It looked like there really might be rats down here. There was no light in the cell; the entire cellblock was lit by a single lightbulb in the corridor. I heard the guard open the door to leave, and then the light went out. It was so black, I couldn't see my hand in front of my face. I lay down on the narrow bunk and stared into the blackness. After a while, my eyes adjusted enough for me to make out that there was a sink and a toilet of sorts, and that was all.

I don't know how many hours I lay there. I must've fallen asleep, because I was awakened by a weird sensation in my pants, near my crotch. It was almost as if tiny claws were scratching at my leg and something was pulling on my pants pocket. Suddenly, I was fully awake and frozen with fear. There was a rat in my pants. Was it going to bite my balls? Slowly, I realized it was gnawing through my pocket to get to those peanuts. Then I heard the cellophane packet rustling and felt peanuts cascading out of the hole in my pocket and into my pant leg. The rat was gobbling them up, tearing my pants from the inside. Then I heard the cellblock door clank open and the light went on. The rat scrambled down my leg and streaked across the floor. It was big and gray and hideous. Then it was gone. The guard came and unlocked my cell.

"Strull, your lawyer is here," he said in French.

XIII

André Berenwald was waiting for me in the corridor outside Inspector Paletti's office. He was a tall, distinguished man in his fifties. He wore an impeccably tailored light gray suit that matched his hair and carried a briefcase. He smiled.

"Eddie?"

"Yes."

"I am André Berenwald. I'm sorry I could not get here sooner, I was…"

"It doesn't matter. I'm glad you're here now. Thank you for helping me."

"Just answer the questions briefly and truthfully. Don't elaborate or volunteer anything. If you are innocent, you have nothing to fear." He knocked on the inspector's door.

"Come," said Paletti from within.

There were two men in the room: Paletti and another plainclothesman, who sat at a separate desk and took notes on a typewriter, typing fast and noisily (a planned distraction?).

Paletti started out. "I am interviewing Edward Strull, age 18 ans, no fixed address, on 10 janvier, 1964. Mr. Strull, did you reside in the building belonging to Mme Sophie Benoit at 17 rue Malebranche last September and October?"

"Yes."

"Didn't you register as 'Jesse Bright?'"

"Yes."

"Why?"

"I'm a writer. That is my nom de plume."

"But didn't you present to Mme Benoit a forged British passport under that name?"

"No, I did not."

"Mme Benoit has testified that you did."

"That's a lie. She thinks I killed her son, so she hates me."

"Did she ever ask to see your passport?"

"No."

"Did you meet her son, Alain Benoit?"

"Yes."

"What did you think of him?"

"I didn't think anything. He was not friendly."

"Did you ever see him go out or come into your building at odd hours?"

"No."

"Did you ever follow him late at night?"

"He already said he never saw Benoit come in or go out late at night," said M. Berenwald indignantly.

"We have a report from the border checkpoint near Geneva that a young man named Jesse Bright crossed into Switzerland on 12 November 1963 with a symphony orchestra from the Conservatoire de Paris. Wasn't that you?"

"No."

"So, it was just a coincidence that there was a British kid named Jesse Bright traveling to Switzerland on that date?"

"Yes."

There was a long pause while he sat and pondered this. Deciding there was no way he could entrap me, he continued.

"Did you know a girl named Martisse Verneuil?"

"Yes." My eyes were getting teary. I had to control myself.

"Did you ever visit her at…" He looked at some scribbled notes he had in front of him. "Number 10 rue des Fossés Saint-Jacques?"

"Yes."

"What was the nature of your relationship?"

"She was my friend."

"Did you know that she was a prostitute?"

"Yes."

"How did you feel when you found out she was murdered?"

I could no longer control the flood of tears that now ran freely down my face. "How do you think I felt?"

"Please answer the question."

"I felt terrible. Very sad."

"And angry?"

"Excuse me, Inspector," said M. Berenwald, "please don't put words in my client's mouth."

"I'll put it another way: Did her murder make you angry at the killer?"

"Yes, it did."

"So, you had a strong motive for wanting to kill 'le tueur de prostituées.'"

"That's not a question," said M. Berenwald.

"Okay. Did you kill Alain Benoit?"

"No."

The questioning went on like this for more than two hours. He established that I had a motive to take revenge on "le tueur de prostituées" and that Alain Benoit most likely was le tueur, and that I had met Mme LaBrot. He showed me police mugshots of Albert and Aziz. I admitted to having seen Albert behind the concierge desk at 10 rue des Fossés Saint-Jacques, but not to actually knowing him. I said I didn't recognize Aziz. Finally, he said:

"So, I submit to you that you either personally stabbed Alain Benoit in the back with Mme Benoit's kitchen knife, or you put Mme LaBrot's henchmen up to it."

M. Berenwald and I spoke in unison: "Prove it!"

M. Berenwald now addressed Inspector Paletti: "Inspector, I now insist that you either charge my client or let him go."

Paletti had no choice. He had no proof, and he knew it.

Outside Paletti's office, several newspaper reporters accosted us. The one from *Le Parisien* had a photographer with him and he snapped my picture. I hoped I looked as bad as I felt so the public could see how the police had mistreated me.

"Monsieur Strull, is Paletti letting you go?"

I let M. Berenwald answer. "Yes. Inspector Paletti had insufficient evidence to arrest my client. He is free and completely exonerated."

"The police were grasping at straws," I chimed in, "I am not guilty of any crime. Go ahead and ask Inspector Paletti. I'd like you to!"

They barged into Paletti's office and embarrassed him, to my great satisfaction.

Back at his office, I thanked M. Berenwald profusely for his help. He did not look pleased but regarded me sternly.

"Now tell me, did you do any of what Paletti said?"

I looked him in the eye but remained silent.

"We have attorney-client privilege here, just like in the U.S."

At last, I spoke. "Someday, I'll write it in a book, and I'll send you a copy. Encore, merci mille fois, Monsieur Berenwald." And I walked out into the Paris streets, a free man.

XIV

The next day, *Le Parisien* had me on the front page again. This time, with the headline: EXONÉRÉ (Exonerated). Other papers carried the story, but not on the front page, and with no photo. This one showed a bedraggled me with a very dapper M. Berenwald at police headquarters. It was just the vindication I was hoping for. I could now walk the streets of Paris with my head held high.

I decided to go see Maurice, my only remaining friend in Paris. I needed to thank him and tell him about my latest adventure. Although I felt like he and I were old friends, I had only met him twice: once at Bert and Jerry's party and once at his office.

His office was at 7 rue Saint-Séverin. Again, I splurged on a taxi. I didn't feel like walking the five kilometers on this cold, damp day. My heart lept as we crossed over the Pont Saint-Michel to my beloved Left Bank.

On the ground floor was Maurice's nightclub, La Grande Séverine. The office of Olympia Press was one flight up. Maurice's secretary, Yvette, was an attractive blonde, about twenty-five. I was flattered she remembered me from my previous visit.

"Bonjour, Jesse. Sa va?"

"Very well—now," I said in French.

She buzzed Maurice on the intercom. "Jesse Bright est là."

I heard Maurice's voice say "Send him in."

There were just the reception area and Maurice's office. All the various functions of operating the publishing house were outsourced to proofreaders, printers, bookbinders, and so on. His inner sanctum had a big window behind his desk, which overlooked the narrow street. There were two guest chairs that faced the desk. The two walls to my right and left were floor-to-ceiling bookshelves, filled mostly with Olympia books in their signature green hardcovers with plain black writing.

"Ah, mon ami, it's been a while," he said, rising to embrace me.

"Yes. It's good to see you, Maurice. As we say in America, 'I owe you big-time'."

"Pas du tout. André called to give me the good news. So, what are you going to do now that you're back?"

Maurice spoke English like a Brit. His father was English and his mother French, so he spoke both languages with native fluency. He had taken his mother's maiden name during the Nazi occupation because his father was a Jew (yep, they're everywhere!).

"I need to finish my journal, which has become a semi-autobiographical novel. I am out of money as usual, so I need to find a way—other than your charity—to keep myself alive until I sell something. I've got to find a place to live and write for no money. Any ideas?"

"How much of a novel do you have?"

"It's about three-quarters done—just the first draft and written by hand. I don't think it's presentable yet."

"I read the first part and it was pretty good. May I see what you have so far?"

"Well… as long as you realize how rough it still is. Okay."

I still had all my possessions with me, so I took out the eight notebooks—they were labeled *Paris Memoirs, 1, 2 3, 4*, etc.—and handed them over. "I hope you can read my scrawl," I said.

He opened the first one.

"I've seen worse. Oh, by the way, I have a letter for you from Annie, and another forwarded to me from your hotel in Amsterdam, I guess from your parents." The one from my parents was not on the usual par avion onionskin; it was a thick, heavy envelope, which seemed to contain multiple pages.

Maurice sat behind his desk and commenced reading. I was very flattered he was making so much time for me. I opened the letter from Annie first. I was dying for news of Kirsten. That was an unfortunate way of putting it. The next moment, I was dying *from* news of Kirsten:

Dear Eddie,

I hope this finds you well. Thank you for your last letter. It was very wise of you to take my advice. As it turns out, Kirsten has moved to London. She met and married a promising conductor, much older than she. My personal opinion is that this was a rash decision and that it will not benefit her career in the long run, but who knows? It might work out. I should be getting a letter from her for you quite soon. I know this must come as a terrible shock to you but, at your age, one is able to withstand such blows and bounce back.

I have your typewriter and sleeping bag. Please telephone me when you get back to Paris to make arrangements to come and get them. Maurice has told me you are a talented writer and that he is helping you. You are lucky to have him in your corner.

Wishing you nothing but good fortune.
Your friend,
Annie

I was stunned. I sat there in a state of shock with Maurice at his desk, pouring over my manuscript. I didn't even open the letter from my parents. I would read that later. I had all the shock and grief I could handle at the moment. I decided I could solve all my problems by killing myself. I would end my memoir/novel with a suicide note. That oughta sell some books. I would leave all the proceeds from the book to my parents to compensate them for all the shock and grief they had endured from me.

"There's some really good stuff here."

"Huh?"

I was still in a daze.

"Jesse. Are you alright?"

"Oh. Sorry. I just got some bad news. Yeah, I'm alright. You like it?"

"Jesse, I think I can provide a place where you can type up this manuscript and finish the novel. I suggest you call it a novel and not a memoir and change the names of the incidental characters. Public figures and dead people are exempt."

"Did you know my real name is Eddie?"

"Oh…yes. Do you want me to call you Eddie?"

"Either one's okay," I said listlessly. "So, you have a place I can work and live?"

"I think so. Give me a few hours. Here's fifty francs, go and get yourself a decent meal. Better change your pants first," he added, pointing to the hole the rat had chewed in my best corduroys near my crotch.

"Oh yeah." I'd almost forgotten about that.

I found a presentable pair of khakis in my suitcase. I thanked Maurice again for his generosity and headed for La Contrescarpe, a sort of greasy spoon that was in the neighborhood of Bert and Jerry's place, near the Panthéon. I didn't want to blow the whole fifty on food. In fact, after hearing about Kirsten, I had very little appetite.

I ordered a cheeseburger and some pommes-frites (French fries). They had a really decent vin rouge and I ordered a carafe which I polished off before and after the meal. This lifted my spirits significantly, but my buoyancy was short-lived.

I opened the letter from my parents. There were two pages handwritten by my father, mostly berating me for disappearing and not telling them where I was. He told me my mother was half out of her mind with worry, crying herself to sleep every night. I had never seen my mother cry even one tear. I guessed there were about fifteen letters from them still waiting for me at the American Express office. The other document was a draft notice from the Selective Service System, ordering me to report for induction into the United States Armed Forces at the Selective Service office at 39 Whitehall Street in lower Manhattan on December 3, 1963. More than a month ago. My father's letter went on to advise me to stay where I was, as I was now officially considered a draft-dodger and fugitive of justice (again!).

They certainly hadn't wasted any time. A month to the day after my eighteenth birthday. Of course, I was aware of that horror known as the Vietnam War that was chewing up and spitting out hundreds of American boys just like me. There was no way I would've participated in that debacle, even if I had been Stateside. So now, I guessed, I could never go home.

Maurice fixed it so I could move back to Annie's to finish the novel. I guessed she felt guilty about being the bearer of such unbearable news. Besides, she had lots of room, and she was hardly ever there.

I used most of the remainder of the money on a cab—I was still schlepping my suitcase and knapsack—and went directly to the Ritz, promising Maurice a completed manuscript within weeks as I left his office.

Annie seemed less than thrilled to see me at her door but welcomed me with muted grace.

"Hello, Eddie. You're looking rather thin. Would you like something to eat?"

"No, thanks. I just ate."

"This came for you."

She handed me a letter from Kirsten. I dreaded opening it. Two bad letters were enough for one day, but at last I did open it:

> *My Dear Eddie,*
>
> *By now you have heard the news that I am married. It was all quite spur-of-the-moment. Colin is a wonderful man, quite a bit older than I and married once before. He is well on his way to becoming a famous conductor. I know this news must hurt you terribly. I'm so sorry. I want you to know, Eddie, that I truly loved you—more than anyone in my life. It is with great sadness that I break this news to you, but the sensible side of me tells me this will be best for both of us in the long run. Please don't hate me. I will always think of you with love in my heart.*
>
> *Kirsten*
>
> *PS: I will be living in London from now on. My return address is on the envelope. Please write and tell me how you are doing from time to time.*

Sensible. How I hate that word. Reminds me of my parents and everything I am not. Too bad; the girl of my dreams turned out *sensible.*

Annie showed me to my new room, which was actually Kirsten's old room where I had spent many a happy night with her before we left Paris.

It brought back sad pangs of memory as I took in the luxurious brocaded bedspread and matching curtains, the signature Ritz cream-and-gold walls, the view of the Place Vendôme. She had set up my typewriter and a ream of white paper on the small, green-and-gold, Louis XV writing desk.

"I will be leaving tomorrow for a two-week tour. I'm trusting you to look after the apartment. No wild parties, eh?"

"Don't worry, all I want to do is finish my novel. There won't be anyone here but me."

"I've stocked the refrigerator and freezer with food. There's canned stuff in the cupboard. Help yourself. Answer the phone if it rings. I've left instructions for the desk to take messages for me and only ring the suite if it's for you."

"Thank you, Annie. I can't tell you how grateful I am."

"This novel of yours…"

"Yes?"

"It better be good."

She gave me a half-smile and left me to it.

The next morning, she was gone when I awoke. I thought about where I was going to go with my story. The last thing I had written was my trip to Amsterdam. Next, I would describe my decision to return to Paris and give myself up to the cops. After that, I would pretty much stick to what really happened. But where will I go next? All the rest will need to be fiction. Do I want a happy ending, or a sad one? If so, what would it be? I was now foundering in uncharted waters. I decided to write a reply to my father's letter instead.

> *Dear Family,*
>
> *I'm very sorry I never got many of your letters. They're probably sitting at American Express waiting for me and I will retrieve them when I have a chance. So much has happened. I returned to Paris, my girlfriend married someone else, and I am now enjoying the luxury of the Hôtel Ritz no less, thanks to the kindness of a friend. I am basically*

surviving on the kindness of friends, and it seems I have only three of them left in Paris.

I now have the shelter and solitude I need to finish my book, which I am doing with all possible speed. I have high hopes that a publisher here will take it, but I have to strike before the river freezes, or whatever that saying is. I must take advantage of the next two weeks to wrap this up so I don't wear out my welcome.

The draft notice does put the kibosh on any plans I might have had to return home. Maybe you could all visit me here. Paris is so beautiful and I would love to show it to you. I speak French quite well now, and I feel very much at home here.

I can't say I'm sorry for what I did; I'm just sorry for the pain and distress I caused you and others. Someday, I hope to redeem myself in your eyes and make you understand why it was so important for me to come here and experience the world on my own. I love and miss you all.

Your not-so-devoted-son,

Eddie

P.S. If you want to write me, please address it to me c/o Maurice Girodias, Olympia Press, 7 rue Saint-Séverin, 5th arrondissment, Paris.

I folded the light-blue *par avion* stationary and put it in its pre-stamped envelope. Then I opened my notebook to my last entry, sharpened a few pencils with my little sharpener (careful to get the shavings in the wastebasket and not on the carpet), and hunkered down. I thought of a few ways the story could turn: 1) My book gets published and I become a big success. 2) My book gets published and I don't become a big success, but Kirsten reads it and leaves her husband to come back to me. 3) I become a big success *and* Kirsten comes back to me. I certainly preferred number three, but would the reader buy it? That's just not the way things happen in real life. Do I want it to be like real life? Well, the whole book up to this point has been based on real life; I just didn't have the time to wait and see how real life would unfold. I had to cast the die right now.

I wrestled with the problem for most of the night, writing it several different ways. Then, I came up with what I thought was an ingenious surprise ending: I finish the book, I put the manuscript in my knapsack and I'm on the bus taking it over to my publisher (a fictionalized version of Maurice). I put the knapsack down on the floor, just for a moment, and a kid grabs it, jumps off the bus, and starts running. I try to chase him, but I lose him. My manuscript and all my notebooks are gone! In the end, the protagonist (Frankie) ends up wandering aimlessly around the Left Bank, mumbling to himself. His mind has been reduced to mush. He becomes a vagrant, sleeping under a bridge. One day, passing a bookstore, he sees his book, his title, with someone else's name on it. But no one will believe he is the real author. The publisher of this book is the same publisher who had read and liked the rough draft. He is the only person who can prove he is the rightful author, but now our protagonist can't get in to see him. In the end, he is murdered in his sleep by a fellow vagrant for his shoes and warm coat. The end. The perfect Dostoyevskian ending. I loved it. I started typing.

XV While typing up my handwritten draft, I found numerous mistakes and lots of room for improvement. I typed the manuscript up twice over a two-week period. My goal was to get an advance from Maurice and clear out of Annie's suite before she got back from her tour. I tied the final manuscript up with a ribbon, the way I'd seen it done by professional authors, and put it in my knapsack. For fear my ending would jinx me, I had made a carbon copy and left that and my notebooks at the suite. I took the further precaution of taking a cab, although I was almost out of money, not a bus or the métro.

I arrived at Maurice's office safely and plopped the hefty stack of paper down on his desk, not without some pride. The title page read: PARIS MEMOIRS: A Novel by Jesse Bright.

The first thing he said was, "Hmm, I'm not sure I like the title."

"Read it first, Maurice. Then, if you can think of a better title, I'll change it. I kind of like that it says both 'memoirs' and 'novel.'"

"Okay, give me a few days. I'll call you at Annie's."

"Please make it fast," I said, "I don't want to be there when she gets back."

Waiting is the hardest activity for me. Patience was a virtue I'd yet to acquire. Maybe I never would. I went out and walked quite a bit. I had no money, so I couldn't buy any clothes or books, both of which I sorely needed.

I found myself at the Palais de l'institut de France on the Left Bank, which housed the Bibliothèque Mazarine, the oldest library in Paris, a 17th century marvel of baroque architecture. It contains, I was told, about 600,000 volumes, many of them original first editions. I found I could select and read from these in the majestic reading room, which was lined with Corinthian columns, marble busts of great writers and scholars of the past, and towering shelves laden with leather bound tomes that reached up to the ceiling forty feet above.

It was mostly scholarly nonfiction works. But somehow I found an early edition of *Justine* by the Marquis de Sade that was dated 1791. I had heard about this and other books by Sade, from whose name comes the word *sadism*, and I was intrigued. As I understood it, all his books were still banned in France, even to this day. How this one sneaked by, I'll never know. Reading in French was never easy for me, and reading in this antiquated French was especially slow going. But my prurient interest drove me on to seek out and decipher the dirty parts. A lot of it reminded me of my Annabelle books.

When I got back to the suite, Annie was there.

"You are still here?" she said, without any greeting.

"Yes. I'm sorry. I was hoping this would all be resolved when you got back. I know I'm *persona non grata* with you, and I appreciate all you've done in spite of that. I finished the manuscript and dropped it off to Maurice yesterday, but I have yet to hear from him. He said it would take a couple of days. If he likes it, I will be out of your hair by tomorrow."

"Okay," she said and headed for her room.

I could tell she was in one of her grumpy moods. Perhaps if I left the paper by her door, her mood would improve by tomorrow.

The next morning, she came into my room and dropped the newspaper down on my bed.

"I see you've made the papers again," she said.

"Yes, but in a good way."

"I don't think any of this publicity is good. Having you staying with me at The Ritz is dragging me into this ugly scandal."

"But this clears me. It says I am completely exonerated!"

"That doesn't make any difference. Don't you see? You're still part of something low and dark and distasteful in the eyes of the people around here, and that reflects on me."

"Alright. I'll leave right now."

I got out of bed and began to pack my bags. I had no idea where I would go and what I would do. I had zero money.

"Here's fifty francs. Get yourself a cheap hotel room," she said, handing me the money.

I didn't want to take it, but I was scared, so I did.

"Thank you for your hospitality and your generosity. I'm…I'm sorry."

And I walked out of the suite and down the carpeted corridor to the elevator. I pushed the button. When it reached my floor, the man slid the door open and I came face-to-face with…

"Robin!"

She looked wonderful. More grown-up, almost glamorous. She smiled her charming, gap-toothed smile.

"Hello, Eddie."

"What are you doing here?"

"Cooper Union offered a year abroad in Paris, and I took it."

"Going down, Monsieur?" the elevator man said, a trifle impatiently.

"Yes. Come on." I grabbed Robin's elbow and dragged her into the elevator with me.

"What's going on? You're moving out?"

"Uh, yes. I'll explain it all when we get outside."

"Here, let me take that." She grabbed the typewriter which I was carrying in my left hand. This freed my left arm for her right arm to hook onto and we walked out into the Place Vendôme arm-in-arm. Suddenly my mood shifted from suicidal to euphoric. My heart soared walking with Robin once again.

"So, where are you studying?" I asked, trying to maintain my composure.

"L'École des Beaux Arts. Et j'apprends un petit peu de Français."

"Très bon!" I said. "L'École des Beaux Arts! You must be quite an artist. They don't take just anybody."

There were several cafés in the Place Vendôme and we sat at an outside table, even though it was quite cold.

"Are you cold? Would you like to move inside?"

"No, I'm fine. This coat is very warm." Then, an abrupt change of tone. "So, what's going on, Eddie?"

"It's a long story and complicated. First, you tell me something: How did you find me?"

"I spoke with your father on the phone. He didn't sound at all happy with you. He told me about the draft notice. So you couldn't go home if you wanted to?"

"That's about the size of it. And I've been in a spot of bother with the law." I unrolled the paper I'd been carrying and placed it in front of her. "It's all here in the newspaper, so no point in trying to keep it from you. This is why my ex-friend Annie kicked me out of the Ritz. Turns out she's just a big snob after all. Afraid of getting tainted by this sordid business."

Robin wasn't able to read the article, so I summed up the whole nasty story, including the part about my "friendship" with Martisse. I told her about finishing the novel and leaving it with "my publisher," whom I was already assuming would publish it.

"Meanwhile, I've got no money and no place to stay."

The waiter came to take our order. "Deux chocolats chauds," said Robin, authoritatively. "Don't worry, I've got money."

"Robin, I couldn't..."

"Hush! I'm taking care of you 'til you get on your feet. When you're a big, important writer, I claim bragging rights."

We both smiled and looked into each other's eyes. It was as if no time had passed.

"I have a place just across the river, right by the school," she said. "My very own *atelier*. I have it all to myself. Wanna see it?"

My whole body filled up with a warmth I hadn't felt in weeks—and it wasn't just the hot chocolate. All my sorrow was now replaced by an inexpressible joy. I didn't feel the cold as we walked through the Tuileries Gardens, the skeletal trees now stripped of their leaves, over the Pont des Arts, and down the rue Bonaparte, right past the École. We turned left at rue de l'Abbaye, a narrow street in the heart of the classy Saint-Germain art district. Several galleries lined the street featuring work by famous artists. 11 rue de l'Abbaye had high, ornate wooden doors and the windows had those little balconies with wrought-iron railings that typified so much of Paris. It was a very high-class building. On the ground floor was a gallery. Robin took me up the ancient "iron cage" elevator to the top floor. Her place was spectacular, a bona fide *atelier* (artist's studio), complete with skylight. It was a spacious loft with a kitchen alcove and a private WC. It smelled like my old art school: turpentine and oil paint. An imposing easel dominated the room, and more than a dozen oil-on-canvas paintings hung or leaned against the walls. Robin had been busy.

"Holy shit! How did you get this place?"

"My parents shelled out for it. They wanted me in a safe neighborhood—and near the school. And after all, it's only for a year."

I spent a few minutes mutely gazing at her artwork. "These are fantastic. You're a truly gifted artist."

Robin turned a lovely shade of red. "Do you really think so, Eddie?"

"Surely you must know how good you are."

"No, I really don't. There are plenty of people at my school who are much better."

"I doubt that. Hey, it's cold in here."

She went to the radiator under the window and turned a creaky steam valve. The radiator started making clanging noises, indicating that the steam was coming up.

"Unbelievable," I said.

"Yeah," she said. "It's got steam heat."

"No, I meant that I found you—you found me—after all this time."

She went to the far end of the room and put a 45 record on the small record player. It was "Hello Stranger" by Barbara Lewis.

"Shall we dance?" she said, opening her arms wide.

Our bodies came together like puzzle pieces. We danced around the room, wrapped in a close embrace, and then we were kissing. She was always a wonderful kisser, but she had improved. The room started spinning. I lost my balance. I literally didn't know which way was up. We landed on the bed and started peeling each other's clothes off. Once naked, we got under the patchwork comforter. Our bodies quickly heated things up under there.

"I take it you're not a virgin anymore."

"Correct."

I reached for my pants and pulled a condom out of the pocket (always prepared).

"No need," she said, "I'm on the pill."

"Say, how many boyfriends have you had anyway?" She looked skyward, as if trying to remember them all, and started counting on her fingers. "Forget it," I said at last, "I don't wanna know." She laughed, happy to get a rise out of me.

"In my heart, there's been only you, Eddie. Will you stay here with me? I have a perfect little desk over there where you can do your writing. I promise I won't bother…"

I stopped her mouth with a kiss. "Yes."

We took our time, exploring each other's body from top to toe. Every nook and cranny. I had never experienced anything to compare with this. Our two bodies became one. We had a simultaneous orgasm. And I had an epiphany: I realized in that brief moment that what we had just shared, that moment of pure joy, was a microcosm of all creation. It's why we're here.

I tried to explain it to Robin, but she just laughed and said, "It was great sex, Eddie. Now shut up and give me a cigarette."

I did as I was told. We shared a Gaulois and some vin rouge.

"How long have you been here?" I asked her.

"Just since the first week in January. The winter term just started day before yesterday."

"You mean, you did all this work in under two weeks?"

"Uh-huh. I have more at school. I've been especially inspired since I got to Paris. For an artist, this place is magic."

"For a writer, too. Although I can't say all my experiences have been as magical as this one." We started to kiss again. Then I remembered to call Maurice. "Where's the nearest telephone?"

She had her own phone, a rare luxury on the Rive Gauche. I dialed Maurice's office and got him on the phone.

"Hello, Maurice? It's Eddie…" He started to tell me about the manuscript. He'd finished reading it, and he had plenty to say.

"Listen…Maurice…yeah, yeah, I know it needs work…I don't like the ending either. Not anymore. Listen, Annie kicked me out. I'm with Robin now…yeah. They don't call me 'Fast Eddie' for nothing…ha-ha-

ha…here's my new number: St. Germain 42-51. Now, you were saying about the manuscript?… I agree completely. I need to rework the ending… yeah, I know I can't kill off the narrator when the whole book is in the first person…he's not gonna die, okay? It'll be an upbeat ending—I don't quite know what it is yet, but it will be…yeah. It'll be sweet... Okay. I'm retyping the whole thing from the beginning. You can keep the draft you have. I have a carbon copy. And I have the title: *Paris Escapade*…you like it? Good! Plus tard, mon vieux." I hung up and turned to Robin, who was still beside me, under the covers, naked. I peeled back the covers, and I started kissing her all over. "Thank you, thank you, thank you, thank you, thank you, my darling!"

"What for?"

"For giving me back my life."

XVI

The next day was a school day for Robin. And it was snowing. I stayed in bed and watched her adoringly. She loaded some books and a sketch pad into a big, canvas shoulder bag, put on a pair of red rubber boots over her shoes, and her warm loden coat with the hood, kissed me, and set off, leaving me alone under the patch quilt, still bedazzled by my amazing reversal of fortune. It was enough to give a guy religion.

I got up, turned on the heat, and made coffee and croissants. Then, still in my PJs and Robin's thick, pink terrycloth robe, I sat at the typewriter and started rewriting my novel from the beginning. I filled in new details that had been absent in the previous drafts. I thought about the great books I had read and how the details made all the difference. I worked and reworked it all morning until my stomach let me know it was time for a break.

I made myself a cold sandwich of a baguette, some kind of cheese, and liverwurst. Washed it down with reheated coffee. As I ate, I mused at how my worldview had changed overnight; how I now had to write this book as if it were a new book, how my joy at being alive had to illuminate all the pages, even the dark ones. I removed some of the fictional embellishments and replaced them with the truth. Some of that true stuff was hard for me to write, and I knew it would make Frankie—my narrator and alter ego—less sympathetic. For instance, I told how the assassination of Alain really took place, how our protagonist puts Mme LaBrot's henchmen up to the crime, changing only the names. I wondered if this could be used against me and the LaBrot gang in court, but since all the names were changed and I even changed "le tueur de prostituées" (The Hooker Killer), the appellation the papers had used, to "le tueur de filles de joie" (The Streetwalker Killer), I figured I could get away with it. I made a mental note to run it by M. Berenwald before submitting a final draft to Maurice. This final draft was going to be a hard slog, especially for the likes of me. I've always squeaked by on my natural brains and talent alone, always taking the path of least resistance. But that didn't work here. To make a great piece of literature—even a good one—takes work. And there's no getting around it, no instant gratification, no feeling of accomplishment, only lingering doubt.

The days went by like this: Cold and dreary outside, me alone with the typewriter inside until Robin came home. Each night, I would show her my new pages, and she would praise my literary prowess to the skies. But this was the girl who loved me; far from an objective reader. When I showed her the parts about Martisse's murder and how I exacted my revenge, she was shocked.

"What I had before was fictional. It let me off the hook. This is the truth," I told her. "I'm not proud of it, but he killed someone I loved and I exacted my revenge."

She just shook her head in bewilderment and said nothing.

"I want your forgiveness," I said.

She said nothing.

"Say you forgive me, *please*."

"It's not for me to forgive you, Eddie. You have to forgive yourself."

I said nothing.

That night was the first night we didn't make love. We both lay there, silently contemplating the ceiling. Finally, I said, "Have you stopped loving me?"

"Never. I couldn't stop if I wanted to."

We embraced, kissed, and fell asleep.

I worked doggedly but without satisfaction for the next two weeks. I had no idea if what I was doing was any good at all, if anyone would even be interested. By February third, I had a typed draft I felt was good enough to show M. Berenwald, and then Maurice. The new ending I'd fabricated projected what I hoped would happen: The girl and the boy spend an idyllic courtship, his book gets accepted for publication and makes him the new *enfant terrible* of the literary world, and they live happily ever after. Well, it's not that simple, but that's the gist of it.

I phoned M. Berenwald and asked if I could make an appointment to consult with him briefly about that one section of my book.

"Remember when you asked me what really happened?"

"Yes."

"Well, I'm ready now to give you the answers. They're in my new manuscript. May I show it to you? It might get me prosecuted."

"Can you be here in an hour?"

An hour later, I was at his office with the manuscript. After reading the salient sections, he regarded me gravely.

"I thought it was something like this. So you decided to come clean, eh—at least within the confines of fiction?"

"Not if they put me in jail for it," I said. "And if Mme LaBrot and her minions get busted, I'm as good as dead. They might kill me anyway, just on general principles."

"Mmm, perhaps. But by doing that they would be admitting their guilt. And you are presenting this as a work of fiction, not memoir, correct?"

"Correct."

"Then they still can't prove you didn't make all this up, just for entertainment value. You can publish it with impunity."

"Can I use your phone?"

I called Maurice and told him I had a finished manuscript. He told me to drop it off with his secretary and he would call me as soon as he'd read it. I took a cab to Maurice's, then walked back to Robin's.

That night, Robin came home in a much better mood. One of her paintings had been selected as part of the "Grand Artistes de Demain" (Great Artists of Tomorrow) exhibition at the Musée National d'Art Moderne (National Museum of Modern Art) in the Palais de Tokyo next month.

"See? I told you," I said. "I know great art when I see it."

She rushed into my arms and we kissed passionately, last night's unpleasantness completely forgotten. I showed her the carbon copy of the finished manuscript and told her I had dropped it off with Maurice this afternoon.

"I got Berenwald's legal blessing. They can't arrest me for fiction."

The three days of waiting to hear from Maurice were unbearable. At last, on Thursday, February sixth, he called and asked if I could come to his office in an hour. It was just a short walk from Robin's place, so I was early. I sat with Yvette in the waiting room after she announced me. He said he would be a few minutes longer. Yvette and I made small talk, speculating about the likelihood of more snow this afternoon. She answered the phone and took messages. One of them was from Vladimir Nabokov. Probably asking where his *Lolita* royalties were. February was royalty month, and as Maurice had said, I might get a few bucks, even after all the advances. My *Annabelle* books were apparently doing pretty well. "Terry Malloy" was, by far, a more successful author than "Jesse Bright."

After fifteen or twenty minutes, Maurice opened the door and asked me to come in. He held up my manuscript as if to prove to me he had indeed read it and then dropped it unceremoniously on his desk. This did not bode well.

"Eddie, I don't know how to tell you this…"

"You don't like it."

"I like it. It's good…it's just not for Olympia. We do avant-garde, controversial. The only shocking thing in this is the unexpected blowjob, and even that isn't very shocking in 1964."

I just sat there and looked crestfallen.

"Barney Rosset at Grove Press in New York might be interested," Maurice continued. "There's a guy there named Seaver who might like it. He translates and publishes a lot of French stuff for them. Maybe the locations and so forth will strike them as exotic enough to take a chance on it. If you like, I can write them a note and send the manuscript to them. You have a copy?"

"Carbon copy. Yes," I said without much enthusiasm. "Sure, send it. I guess it can't hurt."

"Well, this might cheer you up." He handed me an envelope which contained a check for 626 francs and change. "And that's after I deducted your advances. Why don't you write more porno for me? 'Terry Malloy' is very popular."

"That makes one of us," I said. "Okay. I need the money, so I'll write more porno."

I bade him adieu and walked home through the cold, gray twilight. A few flakes of snow were already falling.

XVII

I went home and broke the news to Robin. Over-dramatically, I told her I was a failure as a legitimate author and would now become Terry Malloy, the porno writer. I showed her the royalty check to prove my point.

"I've got to send some of it to my attorney, but the rest I want you to have."

She waved it away. "Don't write porno, Eddie. You're a damn fine writer. How many eighteen-year-olds can say they've written a whole novel? It's a damn fine novel, Eddie. Keep sending it out to other publishers."

"Well, I can do that and write porno for Maurice at the same time. I can't keep sponging off you."

"Why not? I'm sponging off my father. He doesn't mind. He's loaded."

"Oh yeah, the Hamptons. I almost forgot. How did he get so rich, if you don't mind my asking?"

"Ever hear of the law firm Reichenbach, Gurney, and Rothchild?"

"No."

"Well, they're one of the biggest corporate law firms in Manhattan. He's the founding partner."

"I'm still not sponging—off you or him—I'm gonna pull my weight. As much as possible. I'm gonna be Terry Malloy."

She sighed. "Okay, Terry."

"I coulda been a contender. I coulda been somebody, instead of a bum which is what I am, let's face it," I said through my nose, doing my best Marlon Brando, which was only fair.

We both had a good laugh.

"Okay, then. If you're gonna be a porno writer, I think we oughta start doing some research," she said. She started unbuttoning her blouse, slowly and seductively, while doing a slow-motion striptease. I was seeing a new, very exciting Robin. And, once again, I thanked my lucky stars.

"Got handcuffs?" I said. "Maurice likes kinky."

And so, I started a new Annabelle book. This time, I envisioned the new, sexy Robin as Annabelle. For some reason, people love series. If they get hooked on a character in one book, they want to keep reading about the same character in book after book. Personally, I think this is boring. I like to read something new and different every time, but continuing with Annabelle suited my purposes and burnished the reputation of that great porno author, Terry Malloy.

Maurice started forwarding interview requests from somewhat sketchy journalists and radio personalities. There was even a German TV show that wanted me. I refused them all. No way was I going to further burnish Terry Malloy's reputation at the expense of Jesse Bright's.

I worked on *More Erotic Adventures with Annabelle (Book 3)* with all the focus and dedication I would give to my legitimate writing. If I was going to be relegated to the seamy world of porno, I would at least be the king of it (that was presumptuous of me, given that I knew very well that many of the best of the American expat authors were doing exactly the same thing for Maurice to make money).

In this installment, Annabelle is kidnapped by sex-slave smugglers from the luxurious chateau where she has lived happily and comfortably with the kind nobleman who rescued her in the last book. She's put aboard a ship that takes her to North Africa, where she is sold to a cruel warlord and subjected to all kinds of S&M abominations, which she actually gets to like a little. There's even a handsome and sexy Arab prince with some weird proclivities who takes a fancy to her—and vice versa. Meanwhile, her paramour the nobleman marshals all of his resources to find her. So it's part detective story. The one thing all the Annabelle books had in common was that they were a non-stop assault on all of Annabelle's orifices by giant penises. Some of them were benevolent, and some were bent on inflicting pain. Some were not bent at all. Some were made of rubber and wielded by an evil dominatrix. But the one thing they all had in common was that they were all enormous. Sometimes I almost wished she would pity-fuck some guy with a small one, but having been reamed as much as she had, I doubted she would even feel it.

The snow and cold throughout February made it a perfect writing month, and I was able to finish the Annabelle book by the twenty-ninth. It was a leap year. The other thing I did was visit the Librairie Anglaise, a bookstore specializing in English-language books at 42 rue de Seine, right around the corner from Robin's atelier. It was owned and operated by a middle-aged, very attractive French woman named Gaït Frogé. She was quite tall—taller than me—and her beautiful auburn hair was offset by her striking blue eyes and pale skin.

I was looking for publishers that might be interested in publishing my novel. Mlle Frogé was very helpful and friendly, especially when I confided in her that I was Terry Malloy. *The* Terry Malloy. Apparently, her shop was the biggest distributor of Maurice's porno imprint, Ophelia, and she had several copies of both my Annabelle books on hand. I explained to her about looking for a publisher for my legitimate novel and why Maurice had turned it down for Olympia. She had some suggestions, including: Black Sun Press, Faber and Faber, and Obsidian House. But looking at the kinds of stuff they published, I doubted these very highbrow presses would be interested in my distinctly plain-English American style of writing. I resolved to send off some mimeographed copies of my manuscript to them anyway with a carefully worded letter. But Maurice's suggestion of Grove Press still seemed most promising.

After learning who I was, Gaït became very flirtatious. She was completely fluent in English and spoke like a Britisher. She wanted to know if I was a child prodigy. I told her I was eighteen and so qualified as an adult prodigy. Never being able to resist a beautiful face and body, I was sorely tempted. I didn't say no, but left, saying I would stop by again real soon. Then I thought about Robin and how much I loved her, how thankful I was to have her, and how badly I wanted not to fuck this up.

On March 1st, I went to Maurice's office and presented him with *Annabelle, Book 3*. A few days later, I got another advance for 300 francs. His note said he thought it was the best Annabelle book yet and he had gotten a lot of laughs out of it. I guess my weird humor was not lost on him.

I didn't go back to see Gaït. Not right away, anyhow. The temptation would be too great. I wanted to stick with Robin, not only for emotional reasons but also—quite frankly—for material ones. Our comfortable lifestyle, her father's millions, they all contributed to my not-so-pure motives.

She was an artist, and therefore temperamental. I, too, was artistic and temperamental. We often clashed. We both thought we knew best about everything. I don't actually remember the causes of all our conflicts. They were trivial, but when people have intense feelings for each other, they have the power to push each other's emotional buttons, so trivial matters are blown all out of proportion. In retrospect, I wish I had not attributed so much importance to them and had let her have her way. Ultimately, she did get her way on almost everything. She was the one, after all, holding the purse strings. These disputes were always resolved in the same way: Wild, unbridled lovemaking of the highest order. The angrier we were at each other, the more intense our make-up sex. It was a tempestuous affair. Tempestuous and wonderful.

One argument got so nasty, she banished me from her place. I was out on the street again, with no place to go. That's when I went back to see Gaït. She said I could crash at her place, at least for the night. It was right above the shop, not 100 paces away from Robin's place.

Gaït believed in free thought, free expression, and free love. I must confess, somewhat guiltily, that I had a wonderful time with her. I knew it was transitory, that I would go home to Robin as soon as she cooled down, but my tryst with Gaït was a tonic to my fragile ego and a boost to my hungry libido. Besides making love exquisitely, she turned me on to some great books, great food, and great wine. I told her about finding the first edition of *Justine* in the Bibliothèque Mazarine and struggling with the gothic French and she gave me a copy of it in English, published by Olympia in

1953. She was so smart, so beautiful, I wondered why she wasn't married. She told me she had tried it and it wasn't for her.

I called Robin the next day, and we were both all tears and apologies, but I had to conceal the fact that I was in one of the best moods of my life. I stopped and bought her a small bunch of lilacs. When I got home, she asked where I had spent the night. I told her I had slept on the floor of Maurice's office. She sniffed me suspiciously. "Then why do you smell of perfume? Lilac?" Then I produced the flowers and her suspicions were dispelled. Robin's sense of smell was unusually keen. I told her I needed a shower, hastily grabbed a towel and soap and went down the hall to the bathroom. There, I washed the truly incriminating scent of Gaït off my body.

XVIII

On Sunday, March eighth, the "Grand Artistes de Demain" exhibition was to open at the Palais de Tokyo. The day before, Jan and Robert Reichenbach, Robin's parents, flew in. We were to meet them for lunch at the Ritz, where they were staying. I asked Robin not to mention to them that I had stayed there—that we had met there. This would unravel too many questions about me that I didn't want asked. It was enough that we resolved to tell them we were living together.

For the Ritz Bar, we had to wear our best threads. Robin had an assortment of beautiful ensembles she had bought in Paris before school started. I trotted out my white shirt, plain black tie, tweed sports jacket, and black slacks—my only "presentable" outfit, the one I'd last worn to Charlotte's play what seemed like a century ago. I still had the scuffed black loafers, which I managed to shine up enough to pass unnoticed. The weather was still wintery, with patches of snow and ice on the ground. My jacket was scarcely warm enough, but it was a short cab ride, and my shabby overcoat would've spoiled the effect.

The Reichenbachs were already seated when we arrived. They were exactly what I expected: A handsome couple in their forties. He was the very picture of "distinguished": Graying around the temples, clean-shaven, an expensive, conservative suit. She was attractive, in a tailored Channel suit (how appropriate, since Coco Channel had lived in this very hotel), dyed blonde hair, perfect makeup. Everything about them said "straight-laced, American, upper crust." Nothing about them said "Jewish."

As soon as Robin introduced me, the questions started.

Mrs. Reichenbach: "Are you a student, Eddie?"

"Not exactly. A student of life, maybe. I write."

Mr. Reichenbach: "Ever made any money at it?"

"Some."

Mrs. R: "What do you write about?"

"Different things. I write fiction."

Mrs. R: "I'd love to read some of it sometime."

"Sometime perhaps you will."

"I hear this is one of the greatest restaurants in Paris," said Robin, making a game try at changing the subject.

Mrs. R: "It is. We've eaten here many times." She smiled at her husband—a peculiar kind of smile. "Remember, dear?"

Mr. R: "How could I forget?" *Was there a subtext here I wasn't getting?*

Mrs. R: "So, how long have you two known each other?"

Robin: "We met here last summer when I was on that camping trip. Then, when I came to school here, we just happened to bump into each other at the Deux Maggots."

Good story. She didn't tell them about my being on that camping trip and running away. And that tourist trap, les Deux Maggots, was a good touch—right around the corner from Robin's atelier. And now, the million-dollar question:

Mr. R: "Where are you living, Eddie?"

I looked at Robin. "We're living together, Daddy. At my place."

There was an uncomfortable silence.

Mrs. R: "Don't you think you're a bit young for that?"

Robin and I answered in unison: "No."

We met their stares with unblinking determination, and they knew further discussion was pointless.

Mrs. R turned to her husband. "Well, at least he's Jewish."

Just at that moment, a waiter arrived to take our drink orders. I needed one.

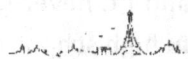

The next day was the exhibition. There was a large turnout, mostly fellow students, but some teachers, parents, and a few journalists.

I was so proud of Robin. As far as I was concerned, her painting—a blurry cityscape of the bridges over the Seine in winter, all shades of gray and white—outshone them all. It was a very large horizontal canvas, and it dominated one wall. It won second prize in the competition (it seems preference was always given to male artists). Robin's friend Claudette told us it was very unusual for a female artist to even place in one of these competitions, so it was a major coup. They gave her a bronze statuette of a muse with her name engraved on a brass plate at the base. The newspaper photographers took photos of her with it, which I was careful to stay out of. I'd had more than my share of publicity.

Robin's parents stopped up to the atelier after the show for a quick glass of champagne to toast her victory and check out our digs. Mrs. R snooped through my book collection and extracted a copy of *The Erotic Adventures of Annabelle.*

"You read this trash?" she asked me.

I wanted to say, "I wrote it," but bit my tongue. "My publisher gave it to me. I've never read it."

They flew out of Orly the next morning. Mr. R had to stop in London on business on the way back to New York. Robin and I got up early to see them off at the Ritz. She was sorry to see them go. I wasn't.

Spring break started for Robin that week, although it still felt very much like winter. We decided to borrow a car from her friend Claudette and take a trip up to the mountains to play in the snow, of which there was still plenty.

It was a cream-colored, 1959 Fiat 500 with a thirteen-horsepower rear engine. There was a joke about those in New York: "Fix It Again, Tony." We resolved to pack light; this thing would have a hard time going up mountains. The closest ski resort to Paris was Le Mont-Dore, about five hours due south. I didn't ski, and I'd never learned to drive. In New York City, there was no driver's ed in high school, but in Long Island, there was. So Robin had to do all the driving. We decided to see if we could rent a toboggan when we got there, or a couple of good old-fashioned sleds.

One of my fondest childhood memories was going to the country in the winter and sliding down a big hill through the woods on a sled. Lying on my belly and steering with the wooden crossbar in front made it seem like

I was going even faster than I was. I hadn't done that in seven or eight years.

In the morning (Tuesday), we set out, heading south on autoroute A6. The closer we got to our destination, the steeper and curvier the road became. And narrower. And icy. To make it worse, the little Fiat would not climb the hill in second gear, and to shift into first, you had to come to a complete stop. By the time we found this out, there was a line of cars, honking impatiently, behind us. We pulled over at the first opportunity and let them all go whizzing by us. Many of them shouted insults and flipped us various versions of the bird as they zoomed past. In first, the car wouldn't go faster than twenty miles (thirty-two kilometers) per hour. Soon, we had a furious line of drivers behind us again. We pulled over and let them go by at every opportunity. But it was, as I said, a two-lane curvy road and very dangerous to cross into the oncoming lane. Of course, some idiot did it. Seeing a car coming toward him around a curve, he jerked his car to the right, slamming into the driver's side of our car. It struck the rear quarter panel. The Fiat skidded on the ice and started spinning. We ended up sitting crossways, blocking the oncoming traffic. It all happened so fast. What I think happened was that the car behind us, which was actually a truck, slammed into the driver's side of the Fiat. Something wet hit the left side of my face. Our car rolled over on its side. My head hit the window. My leg hit the door. Then blackness. Blessed blackness.

XIX

Beth Israel Hospital, New York City, Tuesday, March 17, 1964 (Happy Saint Patrick's Day). My parents and sister came into vague focus standing over my bed. They looked solemn. My right leg was in a heavy plaster cast and suspended over the bed by one of those pulley things. My head was bandaged.

"Am I in New York?"

They nodded.

"Where's Robin?" I asked.

"Shhh. You have to stay quiet, Eddie. You're badly injured," my mother said.

"Your leg was broken in three places," said my father. "And your skull was fractured. You'll be alright, but you have to stay in the hospital for another three weeks."

"*Where's Robin?!*"

They stared at me in grim silence.

"She's dead, isn't she?"

My fourteen-year-old sister Janey flung herself over me, as if to shelter me from a grenade attack. She was crying. Nobody had to say anything more.

XX November 3, 1964, Astor Place, New York City. Happy Birthday to me. I'm nineteen and I feel like I'm ninety. I walk with a cane like an old man. It's a wintery day, reminding me of another wintery day, seven months ago. I'm standing on the asphalt island in the middle of the intersection of Eighth Street, Lafayette Street, and Cooper Square. Right beside me is the Big Black Cube sculpture. Someone has scrawled on it in white chalk: GIVE ME LIBRIUM OR GIVE ME METH. I'm staring at the Great Hall of Cooper Union. I'm waiting for Robin to come out. It's cold, and I know she's not coming, but I'm prepared to wait a long time.

My book, *Paris Escapade*, was published three months ago. They tell me it's selling well, but there's no joy in it for me. The happy ending, in which the boy and girl live happily ever after, went over big. But you and I know that was a made-up ending, written before I knew the real ending. Nonetheless, it's good they're happy together somewhere.

With one leg shorter than the other, I'm no longer the glamor boy, the lady killer I once was. Nor do I care. At the tender age of eighteen, I'd reached the pinnacle of my life. I'd found the girl that made me want no others. It's been straight downhill from there.

Robin's memorial had been held at a posh art gallery on Fifth Avenue several months earlier. I was able to get there, but just barely. At the time, I was in a wheelchair and my sister had to help me get around. There was a blowup of a beautiful photo of her and the walls were covered with her work. A dazzling collection for any artist, let alone one who died at eighteen.

I saw Robin's parents. They gave me a cursory nod, and that was all. I was not asked to speak. I wouldn't have anyway. What I had to say to Robin or about Robin was strictly personal. Between me and her.

A group of students exiting Cooper union passed me on their way to the subway. A pretty girl of eighteen made eye contact and smiled at me. I smiled back. I guess it was a reflex. As she went by, almost brushing against me, she winked.

ACKNOWLEDGEMENTS

Thanks for reading the manuscript and the valuable feedback: Kathy Lubin, The Land of Deborah, Brigid Pearson, Eileen Jennifer Hack

French advisors: Marie-Carole De La Cruz, Chris Begood

Author Photo: Janet Caliri

Lyric Quote: *Hello Stranger*

Words and Music by Barbara Ann Lewis

Copyright © 1963 (Renewed) WARNER-TAMERLANE PUBLISHING CORP.

All Rights Reserved

Used By Permission of ALFRED MUSIC

ABOUT THE AUTHOR

After twenty years trembling on the brink of rock stardom and fifteen years working at record companies, Ted Myers left the music business—or perhaps it was the other way around—and took a job as a copywriter at an advertising agency. This cemented his determination to make his mark as an author.

NOTE FROM THE AUTHOR

Word-of-mouth is crucial for any author to succeed. If you enjoyed *Paris Escapade*, please leave a review online—anywhere you are able. Even if it's just a sentence or two. It would make all the difference and would be very much appreciated.

Thanks!
Ted

Thank you so much for reading one of Ted Myers' novels.
If you enjoyed the experience, please check out our recommended
title for your next great read!

Fluffy's Revolution by Ted Myers

"Brisk sci-fi futurism with a feline star and a positive outlook."

–KIRKUS REVIEWS

www.ingramcontent.com/pod-product-compliance
Lightning Source LLC
Chambersburg PA
CBHW011138100726
47898CB00009B/3027

* 9 7 8 1 6 8 4 3 3 5 9 5 4 *